Welcome to the Kokoro Cat Clinic

Berkley titles by Syou Ishida

We'll Prescribe You a Cat

We'll Prescribe You Another Cat

Welcome to the Kokoro Cat Clinic

Welcome to the Kokoro Cat Clinic

Syou Ishida

Translated from the Japanese by
E. Madison Shimoda

Berkley
New York

BERKLEY
An imprint of Penguin Random House LLC
1745 Broadway, New York, NY 10019
penguinrandomhouse.com

Interior illustrations by Alissa Levy

LIBRARY OF CONGRESS CATALOGING-IN-PUBLICATION DATA
Names: Ishida, Syou, 1975- author | Shimoda, E. Madison translator
Title: Welcome to the Kokoro Cat Clinic / Syou Ishida ; translated from the Japanese by E. Madison Shimoda.
Other titles: 880-02 Neko o shohō itashimasu. 3. English
Description: New York: Berkley, 2026. | Series: We'll prescribe you a cat ; 3
Identifiers: LCCN 2026022779 (print) | LCCN 2026022780 (ebook) | ISBN 9798217191444 hardcover | ISBN 9798217191437 ebook
Subjects: LCSH: Cats | Human-animal relationships | LCGFT: Novels
Classification: LCC PL879.4.S54 N4713 (print) | LCC PL879.4.S54 (ebook) | DDC 895.63/6—dc23/eng/20260504
LC record available at https://lccn.loc.gov/2026022779
LC ebook record available at https://lccn.loc.gov/2026022780

Originally published in Japan as 猫を処方いたします。3, *Neko Wo Shoho Itashimasu.3*, by PHP Institute, Inc., in 2024.

This English translation was first published in the United Kingdom by Doubleday, an imprint of Transworld, in 2026. Transworld is part of the Penguin Random House group of companies.

Publication rights for this English edition arranged through Emily Books Agency, Ltd., and Casanovas & Lynch Literary Agency S.L.

Berkley hardcover edition: September 2026

Printed in the United States of America
1st Printing

Bena

1

Bena

Nakagyō Kokoro Clinic for the Soul. On the fifth floor of a building located east of Takoyakushi Street, south of Tominokoji Street, west of Rokkaku Street, north of Fuyacho Street, Nakagyō Ward, Kyoto.

Since 8 a.m. on Saturday, Fūko Hatta had been wandering narrow streets laid out like a Go board. Knowing the names of the main streets in Kyoto was usually enough to find your way around, even if you didn't know the name of the district. Rokkaku Street was about a ten-minute walk from Kyoto Station on Shijō Street. If she continued on this path, she was bound to reach her destination.

That's what she'd thought, but the building was nowhere to be found. She glanced at her watch—it was almost nine. She'd been circling the same area for nearly an hour now.

Fūko had been born and raised in Kyoto, and while

she'd been to this neighborhood plenty of times to shop, it was rare for her to come here on a Saturday morning. There wasn't much pedestrian traffic, even on the usually bustling shopping streets of Shinkyōgoku and Teramachi. Convenience stores were about the only businesses that were open. At first, Fūko found the emptiness of the shopping district refreshing, and she wandered leisurely, as if taking a stroll.

But soon, her composure gave way to impatience.

What she was looking for was a psychiatric clinic on the fifth floor of some building. She had heard that at this very popular clinic there was a talented and handsome doctor who would take your concerns seriously, no matter how small they might seem.

It was the first time she had considered visiting any sort of mental health facility. After Fūko had posted on her social media that she was feeling a little down, a friend had told her about the Nakagyō Kokoro Clinic for the Soul. The doctor's good looks weren't important. What drew Fūko in was the idea that he might inspire her and give her the push she needed. If she could get a seal of approval from a doctor, surely she wouldn't mess up.

She'd been keen to schedule an appointment, but the clinic's contact information was nowhere to be found.

Her extensive online search yielded nothing, and the friend who had recommended the clinic had only heard about it through secondhand accounts.

So, she thought, she would just have to walk in. She knew that most clinics began seeing patients at nine in the morning, so she figured that if she arrived shortly before opening time, they might squeeze her in between appointments. It was why she'd woken up so early on her day off to make this special trip into the city.

Yet time had flown while she'd been searching for the building. She looked at her watch again: it was already past nine.

Standing in the middle of the street, she felt disappointment washing over her. Could she have got the address wrong?

Shops were beginning to open. Saturday brunch at a café in one of the traditional town houses sounded delightful, but Fūko was not in the mood. Her original plan had been to spend this weekend rehearsing.

As she was about to head back to Gion-Shijō Station, she spotted a small alley between the buildings. It was so narrow that the sun's pale morning rays couldn't reach it. The ground was damp, as if it had rained only on that spot.

She squinted at the back of the alley, where a five-story building stood wedged between two tall structures. At that moment, she was on either Tominokoji or Fuyacho Street, or possibly Takoyakushi or Rokkaku Street. Warily, she decided to explore the alley.

"It couldn't be anywhere around here, could it?"

And yet it seemed she had arrived at her destination.

She must have overlooked it, because she'd felt certain the building would be street facing, and it didn't look remotely how she'd imagined. It was so dark and gloomy for a block that was supposedly home to a popular clinic.

Walking slowly up to the entrance, she noticed that the front door stood open. In the dim light, she could make out a hallway extending toward the depths of the building. From where she stood, it was impossible to tell how many patients might be waiting for their appointments. There was even a chance the clinic might already be fully booked that morning.

No harm in checking, she thought. Fūko began to climb the stairs. There it was: the Nakagyō Kokoro Clinic for the Soul, housed in a unit up on the fifth floor. There didn't seem to be any patients outside the door, which looked slightly grim, with its peeling paint and sturdy metal.

Is this a strictly appointment-only, no-walk-ins kind of place after all?

Feeling resigned, she pulled on the door. Perhaps the metal fittings were loose, because it swung open with just a light tug.

As she poked her head through the doorway, her eyes alighted on a simple and tidy-looking space. In front of her was a small reception window, suggesting the clinic's compactness.

She still could not see any patients. Wondering if they might be farther inside, Fūko craned her neck, then heard the pitter-patter of slippers. A nurse appeared. She looked to be in her mid-twenties, about Fūko's age. Beautiful, with long, narrow eyes and a graceful nose. She had a sharp expression.

"Yes, can I help you?"

"Um, I—"

"You're a patient, aren't you? Please come in," said the nurse, without waiting for a response. She glanced toward the back of the room.

They're probably going to fit me in between appointments, thought Fūko.

She stepped inside, relieved she hadn't been turned

away. She looked around, expecting to find a line of other patients, but there was no one.

Where should I wait for my turn? she wondered, glancing at the single armchair. She pushed open the only door and found herself in a room with a folding chair and a desk with a computer. *This can't be the waiting room.* She gently closed the door.

Then the nurse called out from behind her.

"Yes, that's right. The examination room."

"But I don't have an appointment."

"The patient with an appointment hasn't come yet. Do go ahead."

Fūko felt a little thrill at how easily she would be seen by the doctor. She never imagined that she wouldn't have to wait at all.

Then doubts began to surface.

I walk into a well-known psychiatric clinic, and yet there's not a single patient in sight. Could I have got incorrect information?

What she'd heard from her friend was just hearsay.

"Um, this is a psychiatric clinic, right?"

"I don't know about such things."

"Huh?" Fūko's eyes widened. The nurse didn't seem

to be joking. Her well-defined face showed no hint of a smile. She remained cool and distant.

"Please go in. The doctor will follow shortly."

The nurse exuded an energy that brooked no argument. Her forcefulness confounded Fūko. She stepped into the examination room as instructed. It was indeed a simple room, too sparse for any kind of medical practice.

She sat in the folding chair, waiting. After a few seconds, the curtains in the back parted, and a doctor in a white lab coat appeared. Unlike the nurse, he had a beaming smile.

"Hello there! It's your first time here, isn't it?"

Fūko was momentarily tongue-tied. *Is this the talented and handsome doctor everyone's talking about?*

She wouldn't have called him handsome, exactly, but he definitely had a kind face. His demeanor was friendly, and he spoke with a gentle Kyoto accent. He seemed a bit young to be a renowned doctor, though. *Not more than thirty*, thought Fūko.

The nurse's response had made Fūko wonder if she was in the wrong place. It was a little late to worry about that now, but, feeling uneasy, Fūko asked, "Is this the Nakagyō Kokoro Clinic for the Soul?"

"It is. Cool name, right? Sometimes known as the Kokoro Cat Clinic. My own doctor's name is Kokoro Suda, and I borrowed his name without asking. The real Dr. Kokoro's clinic is just around the back, on the other side of this building. Oh, but don't worry—we're not 'fake' or anything. By the way, how did you hear about us?"

The doctor was the one asking questions now.

Real, not fake . . . what on earth does he mean? Fūko was too astonished to respond.

Noticing her silence, the doctor tilted his head to one side.

"Oh? Can't you remember? Have the rumors about our clinic spread so far that we no longer know their source? Oh no! What should we do? It'll be a huge problem if we become too popular. The rumor mill is churning, isn't it? Churning, churning like crazy!"

"M-maybe . . . ?"

"I *see*. This could well be a problem. Is my clinic *trending*? Well, even if it is, it's just the two of us, nurse and me, running this tiny operation. We're not accepting new patients. On top of it all, I'm currently *extremely* sleepy. I'm—how do you say it?—crepuscular? My eyes fly open at daybreak, so I get drowsy around this time.

But since you've come all this way, I'll make an exception for you. What's your name and how old are you?"

"Err."

Fūko was still tongue-tied.

The doctor narrowed his eyes, unmoving, as if he were straining to keep his eyes open. Surely what he'd said about being sleepy was a joke, but based on how the conversation had been going, she'd assumed he'd been about to turn her away. Yet it appeared that that wasn't the case.

"My name is Fūko Hatta, and I'm twenty-seven."

"What brings you in today, Fūko?"

The consultation seemed to have started. Although it was not proceeding in the way she had expected, the doctor appeared ready to hear what she had to say. Fūko reached into her bag and took out a stack of documents.

She started to feel nervous. *Am I going to be able to explain this clearly enough?* she thought. "So, um, I've blacked out the parts I can't share," she said, finding her words.

She was planning to read from a tablet while projecting the presentation materials, but she had also printed copies as a backup in case of technical issues and had used a marker to carefully redact any details she couldn't disclose to outsiders.

That was to say, almost everything was blacked out.

By the time she had removed the proper names, numbers, and graphs, all that remained were meaningless connecting words.

But without the actual document in her hands, it didn't feel real. Fūko rose from her seat. The examination room was so cramped she ended up looming over the doctor.

"On Monday, I have to give a presentation in front of the president as part of a company competition. Like this, but in an auditorium full of people."

She held her documents and stretched out her arms as if presenting a diploma. The stack of papers nearly brushed the doctor's head.

"Whoa there," said the doctor, ducking out of the way. "You're putting a lot of energy into this. A presentation, eh? That's very cool."

"It's not cool at all."

Fūko pulled back her arms. The room was so small it was almost impossible to have a proper conversation while standing. Besides, she seemed to be getting too worked up. She clutched the papers to her chest and sat down.

"I'm sorry. I'm just so nervous that I got a little over-excited."

"I understand. It's like a switch turns on and the excitement gushes out. It happens to me, too—when that switch suddenly flips, I find myself dashing around the room."

Dashing? In this tiny space?

Fūko glanced around. She could reach the back of the room in two or three steps.

No, he must be joking about this, too. He's just reflecting back what I said to help me calm down. With this doctor, I feel I could share even my most trivial problems.

She loosened her grip on the stack of papers she had been clutching to her chest.

"I work in the Accounts department at a company that deals in miscellaneous goods. A little while ago, the company announced this competition, inviting all employees to pitch new product ideas. I worked really hard on my proposal, and it got selected."

"Wow, that's amazing!"

"Not really. I just made it through to the preliminary selection before the final round. Whether or not my idea is adopted hinges on the upcoming presentation."

The doctor gave a small laugh.

"It's a chance to show off your idea. That's great, isn't it?"

Fūko shook her head.

"It's not great at all."

Since the day her proposal had been selected a month ago, she had felt sick to her stomach.

Even now, her guts churned.

"I hate being the center of attention. Just the thought of presenting solo in front of an audience makes my legs tremble. I wanted to back out, but my manager insisted that, since I'd volunteered, I should see it through to the end. But I didn't volunteer—I only did it as part of my job. I'm not even in sales. A presentation like this is too much for me to handle."

An unpleasant scene began to take shape in her mind.

A dimly lit auditorium. Rows of tightly packed chairs.

A presentation is being projected on the screen, and the person who came up with the idea is speaking.

The company had circulated a memo urging as many employees as possible to attend, if their work schedules allowed. But she had no idea how many people would actually show up.

The wholesaler where Fūko worked was located in

Horikawa Gojo and primarily dealt with office appliances and supplies such as ballpoint pens.

Management periodically solicited submissions for new product ideas from the team. It was part of their job and entirely voluntary, but the competition was treated like a special event. Motivated colleagues looked forward to these competitions, though Fūko had always taken part solely as a spectator. The themes varied annually, but she had been impressed by how seriously everyone—from newcomers to seasoned veterans—approached their presentation. Among the proposed ideas were cute products—toiletries, trinkets, unusual office supplies—all of which she was looking forward to seeing come to life.

It was a different story, however, when you had to do it yourself.

Ever since she had been chosen as one of the finalists, Fūko had been practicing her presentation whenever she found the time. She'd sought a colleague's help with the slide projection, and she had been over her script many times.

The pace of her speech, the volume of her voice, the position of her body, and the time allocated for each section—she'd planned everything meticulously.

"I've rehearsed so many times. And even when I'm at home, all I think about is this presentation."

"You're really dedicated to this, aren't you?"

"Well, if someone as inexperienced as me doesn't do . . ."

Visions of failing miserably in that dimly lit auditorium began to form in her mind.

Her nerves overcome her, and her mind goes blank. She can't get the first word out. Her legs begin to shake. Snickers echo around the room. The president asks a challenging question. She is unable to respond. An executive stifles their laughter, and she hangs her head as tears slide down her cheeks.

Disastrous scenarios were strangely easy to visualize. Images of success, in contrast, were difficult to conjure.

With her anxiety mounting, she was also starting to lose confidence in her original idea. People around her had praised it, but she was now convinced it was childish and uninspired.

"I've been preparing incredibly hard so I won't mess up during the actual presentation," said Fūko. "I've double-checked, triple-checked, and gone over everything with a fine-tooth comb. But I still feel anxious. That's why, as a final push, I'd like a doctor to reassure me that everything is going to be fine. I need that stamp of approval to put me at ease." Her fingers clenched around the documents in her lap, crumpling them.

She had already asked her friends and family for guidance. Everyone had said that all that mattered was that she did her best. She'd received various pieces of advice, like drawing the character for "people" (人) on her palm and "swallowing" it to dispel nervousness; an aunt had even suggested imagining everyone in the audience as pumpkins. She had also encountered these tips in the many business self-help books she had inhaled.

But people were not pumpkins.

"I'm deeply moved," said the doctor, a completely serious expression on his face. His previously gentle demeanor had vanished. He pinched the bridge of his nose, looking up at the ceiling as if he were holding back tears. "I'm so moved that my nose is about to run. You double-checked, triple-checked, and reviewed everything repeatedly—you are truly remarkable. You went over it, again and again, with an extra-sturdy, super-fine-tooth comb of the highest-quality chrome that glides through any knots and tangles."

The doctor swung around to his computer and began typing away on his keyboard.

"A tremendously remarkable one . . . Would a little bite be okay?" he asked.

"Little bite?"

"Yes, a little bite. But if you get seriously bitten or scratched, please make sure you go to a clinic, okay? A real one, that is."

"A *real* one?"

As Fūko sat pondering, the doctor suddenly flashed a smile.

"We'll prescribe you a cat. Chitose! Please bring the cat!" he called out toward the curtains at the back.

The nurse, the one Fūko had seen earlier, appeared. In her hands was a plastic pet carrier.

"Dr. Nikké, should I include some bandages for her just in case?"

"Oh, that might be wise. Let's give her the full set."

"Understood!"

The nurse placed the pet carrier on the desk and retreated.

Fūko creased her brow in puzzlement. *Bandages? The full set?*

The doctor clicked open the carrier door and reached inside.

A cat with a long, slender body slunk out.

White fur, dusted with cocoa powder.

A dark-chocolate face.

Fluorescent blue eyes that shone like Christmas lights.

"Is that a . . . Siamese cat?"

"Yes. A beauty, no?"

Perhaps the carrier had been a bit snug; the cat placed its front paws on the desk and raised its rear in a contented stretch. Its body was a pink-tinged white. It had tall, triangular ears; its tail was a deep brown. Its front and hind legs displayed the gradient of dark wood, deepening toward the ends.

And—those paws.

They looked as though they had been dipped in a chocolate fountain.

"*Adorable.*" The word slipped out of her with a sigh.

Her company's miscellaneous goods often featured animal motifs, with cats being by far the most popular. There were cat mugs, cat masking tape, phone cases, towels, and pouches. Most items showcased illustrations or line drawings of cats, while some had actual photographs printed on them. They featured a variety of different breeds, and the Siamese, with its stylish coloring, frequently appeared on items targeted at adults.

Seeing one for real was a totally different thing.

Fūko felt herself falling for the cat's charm. Its short, silky fur appeared remarkably soft. Its face was so petite, accentuated by deep brown markings reminiscent of contouring makeup. Daintily set in the middle was a pitch-black nose.

A true beauty. That's the only way to describe it.

Since it's a cat, should it be called a true feline beauty?

With one hand over her mouth, Fūko reached out, moving slowly to avoid alarming it.

In the next moment, her hand was met with a slap.

"Ouch!"

The doctor snorted.

Fūko was not sure what had just happened. She reflexively withdrew the hand that had been struck with such force and hunched her shoulders. It hadn't hurt enough for her to cry out, but it had certainly taken her by surprise.

She had just been slapped. By a cat's chocolate-colored front paw.

It was as if she had been scolded for stealing from the cookie jar.

"There was a real snap to that punch. Very cool. You

got right into it. This one might not just go over the knots with a fine-tooth comb. It might tear them right out."

The doctor seemed to be in high spirits, and utterly oblivious.

"So, when is this presentation thing you mentioned happening?"

"The day after tomorrow . . . on Monday."

"Perfect! In that case, please take this cat for the next three days. I'll write you a prescription, so pick up the necessary items at reception." The doctor took hold of the cat around its shoulders with both hands.

In an instant, the cat spun around, giving his hand a big wallop. The doctor widened his eyes in surprise but then broke into a laugh.

"You're a feisty one! All right, all right, now let's get back inside . . ."

He reached his palm around the cat's belly, but before he could even get his hand underneath, it slapped him again.

Twice.

"Ouch!"

The doctor swiftly withdrew his hand. The back of it was turning red.

"Haha. What are you doing, cat? Come on, get inside. Save your slapping for my patient, not for me."

The cat, however, chose to do its own thing, extending its front paw and batting at the doctor's arm in a remarkable barrage of strikes.

"Ouch! Hey! What are you doing? Please stop!"

The cat thumped the doctor on the head and cheeks over and over like a drummer. It had been sitting with its bottom on the desk, but it had now sprung up and was skillfully balancing on its hind legs and tail.

Fūko was once again tongue-tied. The examination room had become some kind of boxing ring. The doctor was getting beaten up mercilessly.

"Ouch! Ouch! Help! Chitose, please help me!"

"What on earth do you think you're doing?"

The curtains flew open, and the nurse strode in. In an instant, she had scooped up the cat, placed it swiftly back in the carrier, and secured the door. She glared at the doctor with narrowed eyes.

"Dr. Nikké, could you please stop playing around in front of the patient?"

"I wasn't playing around. I was getting pummeled!"

The doctor's hands, as well as his cheeks and the tip of his nose, were scarlet and covered in small scratches.

"Ow, that really hurts."

"Oh, don't be so dramatic. Look, now you've startled the patient with that bright red face of yours." She turned her gaze to Fūko, who sat dumbfounded.

"I'll give you what you need at reception, so please come around," she said, thrusting the carrier with the cat toward Fūko.

Fūko took hold of the carrier uneasily. When she glanced across at the doctor, he appeared to be on the verge of tears. *What on earth is going on in this place?* Just moments ago, he had been talking about being so sleepy or else dashing around the room—maybe those hadn't been jokes after all. *He's definitely not normal.* In a panic, Fūko ran out of the examination room.

The waiting room was deserted, and the chair stood empty.

At this very popular psychiatric clinic, there's a handsome doctor who takes your concerns seriously, no matter how small they might seem. When a rumor was repeated often enough, it was hard to tell what was true anymore.

"Ms. Hatta, over here, please."

A pale hand waved; it was the nurse beckoning her. Her face, peering through the reception window, was not looking friendly.

"Here are some supplies. There's an instruction leaflet inside, which I advise you to read carefully. I've also included some bandages, so do use them as needed. But if you are seriously hurt, please be sure to seek medical attention."

"What do you mean, 'seriously hurt'?" asked Fūko, her face stiffening.

The nurse glanced up at her.

"You saw what happened earlier, didn't you? That was just the beginning."

Fūko shuddered.

"The doctor just now—Dr. Nikké—he seemed like he was crying. Is he okay?"

"He'll stop crying before his next patient comes. But thank you for your concern. Now, take care."

Take care? "Well—"

"Take care."

The nurse assumed a composed expression and refused to make any more eye contact. When Fūko had asked if this was a psychiatric clinic and the nurse had answered, "I don't know about such things," maybe she hadn't been joking either.

If this wasn't a mental health clinic, what type of clinic was it?

Was it even a proper clinic?

Holding the cat carrier in one hand and the bag with the various supplies in the other, Fūko took a moment to survey the waiting room one last time. The nurse had mentioned that a patient with an appointment was due.

The room remained empty.

As the Keihan Line train rocked gently, Fūko felt the full weight of the cat on her lap. The express trains bound for Osaka were always crowded, but the local train, which stopped at every station in the residential neighborhoods and so ran at a leisurely pace, was relatively empty.

It was now late Saturday morning. As soon as she became aware of the time, thoughts of the events that would unfold on Monday started creeping into her mind.

It had been five years since she'd joined her company, which distributed a range of products, mainly stationery and office supplies. Some products were made in-house. Although she did clerical work, she occasionally saw the merchandise, and if she liked something, she would buy it at her employee discount.

Fūko considered herself a dedicated worker. She'd made a few mistakes, but never anything too serious, and she got along well with her colleagues and bosses.

As for the competition, she'd only entered it because there had been a strong push for everyone to participate, and she hadn't done so with any hopes of winning. She had simply developed a random idea she'd had for some stationery—something she thought would be nice to have—into a polished presentation. Somehow, it had been selected to go through to the final.

Looking back, she wished she hadn't taken so much trouble over it.

She got off at the Fujinomori stop, and as she went to retrieve her bicycle, which she'd left in front of the station, a realization struck her: *I'm carrying too much stuff.* She had the cat supplies given to her by the nurse—dry food and a litter tray—and the carrier with the Siamese in it was also quite heavy. Her own bag was awkwardly strapped across her back. Trying to ride a bike with all that would be reckless.

Giving up on the idea of cycling, she decided to walk home. She crossed the canal and entered the shopping arcade—though calling it an "arcade" was generous; it had no roof and was just a street lined with mom-and-pop stores. At one time, there had been plenty of shops, but many had gone out of business, giving way to apartment buildings.

It was empty even now, on a Saturday afternoon.

She always rode her bike, so she was walking through her neighborhood for the first time in a long while. She was finding it quite refreshing.

Look at that butcher frying croquettes out on the sidewalk.

Didn't that use to be a clothing store? Now it's a café.

A vacant lot. What was here before?

She hadn't been down this street in ages, and it had declined noticeably since she'd last been here. As a local, she knew she really ought to support these shops. Still, even now, when she'd need cat supplies, the first place that came to mind was the large supermarket on the other side of the train station, where she went whenever she had any shopping to do.

She suddenly stopped in her tracks.

A faded awning caught her eye. Once a bold red, it was now the color of rust. Even the shop name on the awning was faded: TAKATŌ DOG AND CAT GARDEN.

Takatō Dog and Cat Garden was not a chain store or a fancy shop like you might find downtown—it was the sort of pet shop that had been here in this spot for as long as anyone could remember. She passed it almost every day on her way to the station, but it had blended into the scenery and never caught her eye. *It's still around*, she thought, nostalgia washing over her.

A man in an apron stepped out of the white van parked in front of the store. He glanced over at her before disappearing into the shop.

Fūko recognized him immediately: it was Kinnosuke Takatō, her old classmate from elementary school.

Kinnosuke's father owned the shop. Fūko had been inside just once, back in second grade. For her—whose father had a regular office job—a family-owned pet store was a novelty, and on top of that, visiting a boy's house had felt like a huge adventure. She remembered how her heart had raced.

Kinnosuke had been in the group of popular kids at school. She couldn't recall exactly how she came to visit his family's store, but he likely didn't remember her at all.

Once they had moved up grades and been placed in different classes, they didn't talk again. At their local junior high, their paths had hardly ever crossed, and she had no idea which high school he went on to. She thought she'd heard that he went to a university in Tokyo. For a long time, Fūko had treasured the memory of visiting the popular boy's house, but at some point she had forgotten all about it.

Ah, I see. Kinnosuke must have come back to Kyoto and taken over his father's store.

Thanks to having to walk because of her heavy bag and pet carrier, she had run into an old friend. She felt warm with nostalgia, but she also felt a bit sad that he hadn't noticed her.

As she passed the storefront, her heart a little heavy, the glass door slid open.

"Fūko? Fūko Hatta, right?"

Fūko was startled.

Kinnosuke smiled. "Wow, it's been a while—no, more than a while. Ten years? Maybe more. You haven't changed at all."

"Neither have you."

Drawn in by his easygoing manner, Fūko returned his smile. He really hadn't changed one bit—just the same boy, grown into a man.

"Are you still living in the old neighborhood, Fūko?"

"Yeah. I live with my folks. So, you've taken over your father's store, huh?"

"Ah, my father got sick, and I had no choice but to come back from Tokyo."

"Oh, I see. That's really good of you—taking care of your father."

Fūko remembered Kinnosuke's father. When Fūko came to visit, he'd been seated behind the counter in the cramped store and had given her a cursory glance, then ignored her. Because he ran a pet store, she'd assumed Kinnosuke's father would be a kind, animal-loving man, so his coldness had come as a surprise. She'd found him intimidating and stern.

"Is that a cat?"

Kinnosuke peered into Fūko's pet carrier. Perhaps alarmed, the cat shrank back.

Fūko was holding the carrier securely with both hands, but she almost dropped the bag of supplies and her own bag.

"Yeah, it's a cat."

"Taking a cat for a walk? You're carrying a lot of stuff for a casual stroll."

"Um, well . . ." She hesitated. What would a classmate she hadn't seen in years make of a cock-and-bull story about being prescribed a cat at an odd mental health clinic? He might smirk and think she'd turned into some whimsical, airy-fairy type.

"Your house is further up, right? Your bags look heavy. Want me to give you a lift in my van?"

"Really? That would be great."

"Sure. Give me a second. I have to put away the stock I've just taken in. You can wait inside if you like."

Just like he had in second grade, Kinnosuke opened the door wide and welcomed her in. As Fūko was about to enter, she realized something.

"Ah, I can't go in!"

"Why not?

"I've got a cat," said Fūko, holding up the carrier.

Kinnosuke tilted his head in confusion. "Yep, it's been here the whole time."

"I mean, this one's a bit rambunctious. If it messes with your store's fish or something, it'll be a disaster."

"Oh, that's what you're worried about. It's fine. We don't stock live animals anymore."

Kinnosuke gave a bright laugh and opened the door wider.

It was more cramped inside than Fūko remembered, yet surprisingly orderly. In the past, the shelves had been lined with tanks filled with tropical fish and cages holding small birds. She recalled it being dusty and noisy.

"That must be heavy. Why don't you put it down over there?"

Kinnosuke pointed to the counter, and she was happy to put the carrier down. *Thank goodness!* Her arms had been nearing their limit. Glancing around the store, she took in the steel racks, the products on them neatly arranged like in a hardware store. Amused by her surprise at the store's new look, Kinnosuke chuckled.

"Back when my old man was running the place, we had small animals and tropical fish, but taking care of living things is a ton of work. Since I took over, we've stuck to selling pet supplies. How about you, Fūko? What are you doing these days?"

"I work in an office. I handle admin tasks in Accounts."

"I see. Funny how we both live here but haven't bumped into each other."

As Kinnosuke spoke, he took bags of dog food from a large cardboard box, organizing the pet supplies for sale. Various bags and cans of pet food already lined the racks.

But the animals were missing. She hadn't thought

about the store in years, but seeing the shop transformed upset her.

As she'd strolled along the street, it had struck her how difficult things were for small businesses. There were hardly any passersby, let alone customers. Would anyone come to buy those freshly fried croquettes before they went cold?

She thought Kinnosuke was wise to stop selling live animals. While Kyoto boasted many tourist attractions, its population was steadily shrinking.

"Mind if I take a quick look at your cat, Fūko?"

Having finished putting the new stock out, Kinnosuke wiped his forehead with his apron. He leaned his face toward the carrier on the counter.

"What a beautiful cat! You must be particular about its food. What are you feeding it?"

"Umm—"

"A Siamese, right? How old is it?"

Fūko was stumped. *Oh, right, there's an instruction leaflet.* As she rummaged in the paper bag, Kinnosuke opened the carrier's door and lifted the cat out, one hand under its arms, the other supporting its rear.

"Siamese are a well-known breed, but you don't see them around much. I really like them, though."

Fūko pulled out the leaflet. She gave it a quick read, then frowned.

"That cat's not a Siamese, Kinnosuke."

She handed him the leaflet.

> **NAME:** Bena. Male. Five years old. Maeo Thai. Feed a moderate amount of cat food morning and night. Water bowl must always be full. Clean kitty litter as needed. Generally, he can be left alone without any problems. Similar aspects of behavior may have different meanings. Please work out the underlying cause of any behavioral aspect to decide whether it is permitted or should be stopped. That's all.

Bena had refined features, and only the center of his face was dark brown. He looked just like the pictures of Siamese cats on novelty goods and in photos, so Fūko had assumed he was one, too, but evidently, she had been mistaken.

"Apparently, he's a Maeo Thai. That's the first time I've heard of it. Must be a rare breed."

"A Maeo Thai is the same thing as a Siamese. That's just what they're called in Thailand, their native country," said Kinnosuke.

"Oh, really?"

Bena, who had been so unruly at the clinic, was now quietly nestled in Kinnosuke's arms. He was the perfect image of a Siamese: elegant and poised.

"Impressive, Kinnosuke. As the son of a pet store owner, you know your stuff."

"Seriously, Fūko, how can you not know what breed your cat is?"

"Ah." Fūko averted her gaze. It was difficult to explain. "Actually, this isn't my cat. I'm looking after it for a friend, and I'm on my way home with it."

"Oh, I see. That explains why you're carrying all this stuff."

Kinnosuke leaned in close to the cat. Bena looked up, and their noses touched.

"Hmm. He's slender but muscular—looking good. Exercise is essential for cats, too. Just like humans, it's not only about diet. I wonder if there's some product that could give them a workout in less time. There's a cat boom right now, so a good idea could really take off."

"Oh, really?"

The phrase "good idea" made Fūko's heart skip a beat. She forced an awkward smile.

"I've been selling pet supplies online and, surprisingly, the high-end products tend to sell first, particularly the imported ones. The pet market is booming, and if you play your cards right, there's good money to be made. As for the cats themselves, rescues are all the rage, and people are moving away from pedigree breeds or store-bought pets, but the amount of money they spend on their care keeps going up. It's essential to monitor these trends carefully and adapt quickly."

"Wow. You sound like an entrepreneur."

"While I was in Tokyo, I launched a company with a friend."

There was pride in Kinnosuke's voice. Fūko had thought he looked like the same boy, just grown into a man, but now any hint of youth was gone and he suddenly seemed his real age.

Running a small business was probably tough, and it was good to be ambitious. Fūko was reminded of her own job. When she got home, she'd have to go over her presentation again. The competition was in two days.

Out of nowhere, Bena struck Kinnosuke on the chin.

"Ouch!"

Kinnosuke pulled away, but Bena continued to pummel him.

"B-Bena! No! Stop!"

"Ouch!"

Kinnosuke leaned back, pulling his face away from Bena. The cat's front paws remained tense and poised within striking range.

"Fūko, the carrier—can you bring it over?"

"R-right. Sorry!"

Tilting the carrier, they managed to push Bena in tail first. He seemed agitated but backed in smoothly, much to Fūko's relief. It was then that she noticed Kinnosuke's jaw had gone red.

"I'm so sorry, Kinnosuke."

"Nah, I let my guard down. Been a while since I was beaten up like that. That's cats for you, huh?"

Kinnosuke winced with pain, but there was a hint of amusement on his face.

"Did you use to have a cat?" Fūko asked.

"Yeah, back at my parents' place. Got smacked around all the time for no reason. With cats, you can never tell what they're thinking. Oof, it hurts!"

"I have some disinfectant and bandages."

Fūko had been given a complete set for just this situation. As she dabbed disinfectant on Kinnosuke's scratches, he clenched his teeth—it must have stung.

It felt strangely surreal. A place that had once teemed with small animals felt eerily empty without them. But as she tended to the wounds of her classmate, who had been smacked around by a cat, it felt as if she had journeyed back in time.

"You really haven't changed at all, Fūko," Kinnosuke murmured. Fūko didn't know why, but he sounded a little sad.

Kinnosuke gave Fūko a lift home in his minivan. He had given her some canned cat food that was nearing its expiry date. It looked fancier than some food you'd offer to a human.

When Fūko walked in with Bena, Fūko's parents were stunned. They exchanged looks and walked slowly toward the pet carrier.

"Oh wow, it's a cat," said her mother. "The kind you'd find at a rich person's house."

"The kind an oil baron would have on his lap," said her father.

"No, no. Oil barons have cats with longer fur."

"Ah, then maybe in a house with a piano?"

"There are pianos in normal houses, too. Mr. Konishi next door plays late into the night. Isn't it more like one of those cats that gaze out of a window in Western-style mansions?"

"Oh, you mean from a bay window. Houses with bay windows are usually owned by rich people."

Her parents were putting on their best cheerful faces, but she sensed their hesitation. They were probably trying to buy some time by distracting her with conversation while they thought things through. Their daughter had brought home a strange cat. If her parents flat-out refused to let her keep it, it would be over.

"Mom, Dad, can I keep this cat until Monday?" asked Fūko.

Her parents' faces lit up with smiles. They were evidently relieved. "Oh, you're just looking after it for a while! You had me worried there. I didn't know what we'd do if you'd wanted to keep it long term. Right, honey?" her mother said.

"Exactly! You can't just casually decide to have a pet. For one thing, you wouldn't be able to travel," said her father, leaning closer to the carrier's door with obvious delight. "How are you going to manage it, Fūko? It's not going to be easy, taking care of it."

"I'll keep him in my room. I've been given everything I need," Fūko replied.

Without warning, Fūko's father popped open the carrier door. Before Fūko could stop him, Bena was emerging.

He stuck his butt in the air again and stretched. *Shoot!* Fūko panicked. What if he smacked or scratched her parents?

"Dad, this cat's a bit cheeky. So, um, don't touch him, okay?"

Before Fūko could push him back into the carrier, Bena gave her father's knee a gentle tap with one paw.

"Whoa. The cat just reached out and touched me. He *is* cheeky!"

"Hey, what about me!"

Fūko's mother slid over on the sofa, pressing her knee against her husband's.

"Come to Mommy, kitty."

This time, it was Fūko's mother's knee that Bena tapped.

"Wow, he really is cheeky," she said. "What a friendly cat."

"Um, yeah."

Fūko watched warily. Bena was gently tapping her

parents with his paws—technically, you could say he was smacking them.

Her parents didn't reach out to the cat but allowed him to do as he pleased. So far, Bena's movements had been cautious, but he could strike more violently at any moment. Fūko observed him nervously as he sauntered around the living room, then lay down on his side by the sunny window. It seemed he had already lost interest in them.

Fūko's dad headed off for his regular weekend pastime of pachinko, leaving Fūko and her mom at home.

"What about his food?"

Fūko took the supplies out of the paper bag and arranged them on the coffee table. She also took out the three cans she had been given by Kinnosuke. In the course of the drive home, he had taught her many things.

"The bag contains dry food. All I have to do is put some in a dish and give it to him twice a day—once in the morning and once in the evening. If I leave water in a dish, he'll help himself. I'll prepare a meal for him now."

While she was speaking with her mother, Bena had approached without either of them noticing. He was pawing at the three cans that had been stacked up on the table.

That was when Fūko really noticed the cat's eyes. *What an incredible shade of blue!* It was a wonder that a creature with such eyes existed.

Her mother, too, seemed completely smitten.

"I think the kitty is saying he wants that food."

"Yeah, looks like it. But I can't give him the good stuff right away—"

With a loud clang, one of the cans went flying. It landed on its side and rolled across the floor with a clattering sound.

Fūko and her mother froze.

Bena had smacked the can with his paws. He looked over at Fūko again.

"I think the kitty is . . . angry?"

"Y-yeah. But I can't give him the good—"

With another clang, a second can fell to the floor—a quick jab, powered by a whip-like flick of the wrist.

If a cheek had been on the receiving end of that, it would have been pretty painful. Even Fūko's mother, utterly charmed a moment ago, now had a strained look on her face.

"Look, he does seem pretty angry. Wouldn't it be better if we just gave him the canned wet food? Are we not supposed to?"

"No, it's not that we're not supposed to, but if we give him the tasty stuff first, he might not eat the dry food later."

The last can plummeted to the floor. It landed on its side and rolled across the room.

Bena's round, baby-blue eyes were fixed on Fūko and her mother. He looked utterly confident that he'd get what he wanted—the tasty food—not the least bit pleading.

"Wait a second, Bena. Let me ask."

Thank goodness I exchanged contact details with Kinnosuke.

Fūko had been thrilled to reconnect with an old friend and hoped to stay in touch, but she'd never anticipated that they'd be in contact again so soon.

When she called, Kinnosuke laughed and offered some helpful advice.

"All right, I've been told we can give him the canned food. I'll just mix the dry with the wet food," Fūko said to her mother afterward.

"Oh, really? It's your lucky day, kitty. We're going to whip up a delicious meal for you."

They looked it up online and prepared a mix of dry and wet food. The wet stuff resembled watery canned tuna and, unsure of the correct portion, she added the whole can.

Bena devoured the food with such gusto it was satisfying to watch. *But all this fuss over one meal . . .* The wet food he hadn't eaten had to be thrown away. Fūko would have to keep an eye on his appetite when preparing his meals.

Fūko's mother chuckled as she washed up the dish and empty can.

"Pets are hard work after all, aren't they? I find myself wishing for a cat now and then, but I think it might be more trouble than I'm ready for."

Fūko's mother was mild-mannered and prudent, like her daughter. She was not the kind of person to act on impulse just because she found something cute. They had never had a pet before, so they could only speculate about the challenges of caring for one. If it appeared daunting in their imagination, the reality would likely be trickier still.

Fūko's father returned from the pachinko parlor.

"Where's the cat?"

"Honey, you're back early. Did you lose?"

"Yeah, I guess so. The cat? How is he?"

"He's just eaten. He seemed really angry and wouldn't settle for anything but canned food. Right, Fūko?"

"Yep. He was swatting things left and right."

That was true. Bena's gestures in demanding wet food had been pretty forceful.

Fūko's parents sat on their knees, smiling from ear to ear, watching as Bena sauntered over to give them another tap on the knee. It was as if he were using his paw pads as a stamp.

Come to think of it, the instruction leaflet had said something about this: "Similar aspects of behavior may have different meanings. Please work out the underlying cause of any behavioral aspect to decide whether it is permitted or should be stopped."

Indeed, each one of Bena's gestures seemed to have a distinct meaning. The harshest had been when he'd pummeled the doctor—the cat had been fighting him for real. With the cans, it had seemed less like an attack and more of an appeal. And now, when he reached his paw toward her parents, there was a sense of playfulness.

What about that moment with Kinnosuke? Had Bena's punches meant something then as well?

After dinner, Fūko carried Bena to her room. She

managed to pull him into her arms, but, wary of a surprise swipe, she turned her face away from him as much as possible. Once she had released him into her room, Bena wandered around, rubbing his flank on the walls, then slunk behind the curtains.

Fūko was keen to learn more about cats and to understand what lay behind their play. She'd never really thought about having a pet, but she envied families who had one. She suspected—though this was only speculation—that people who lived with animals held them in a particular kind of affection, different from how people felt toward humans and comprehensible only to those who had pets.

And once you'd felt it, your sense of what mattered might be altered—though whether it would be for better or worse was anyone's guess.

Time was getting on now, and Fūko had things she absolutely had to do—in particular, she had to rehearse her presentation.

"Okay, I got this!"

She psyched herself up. There was no monitor, no microphone—yet she could envision her room as a vast venue. Her slides were simple and visually appealing, and on the day of the presentation, she planned to explain everything for her audience.

She dropped her gaze to the floor and began to picture a pumpkin.

Everyone here is a pumpkin. I'll read my script to the pumpkins. As long as I don't make any mistakes, I'll be fine.

She read aloud from the script on her tablet several times, but she still couldn't stop worrying about it. No matter how much she practiced, rehearsals were just rehearsals. It wasn't the same as the real thing.

She lay down on her bed and closed her eyes. She tried visualization, but all she came up with was an image of a lonely dais.

An unpleasant scene began to form in her mind.

Nervous, agitated, and at her wits' end. Cold sweat dripping, legs shaking, tears flowing.

"Tears are a bit much."

She let out a chuckle and opened her eyes. A chocolate cake with triangular ears filled her vision.

She sat up in alarm.

"Oh my goodness, you scared me, Bena."

Bena's face didn't so much as flicker. He just sat primly on the bed. It was amazing how cats could get so close without making a sound or alerting you to their presence. He stared at her with his fluorescent blue eyes. She couldn't help giggling.

"What is it, Bena? Do you want to hear my presentation?" She paused. *Maybe that's not such a bad idea.*

"Bena, stay there."

Fūko swung her legs onto the floor, powered on her tablet, and scrolled back to the first page of her script. She glanced at her bed to check on her audience—there lay Bena, majestically sprawled out, his chocolate-colored tail swaying from side to side.

"Great. You're so dignified it's as if the president himself were here."

I'm going to practice as if the president is really here.

Tablet in hand, Fūko began reading her script, picturing the slides projected behind her. After so many read-throughs, she no longer stumbled over the words. She'd more or less memorized the script, so everything flowed smoothly—

Whack—she felt a sharp smack on her leg.

The words froze in her throat. Bena sat at the edge of her bed. He had just hit her.

"What?"

The blue eyes did not respond to her question. *Maybe I'm making too much noise, and he wants to sleep? Oh, well.*

She began reading aloud again.

Whack—a sharp smack on her leg.

Whack, whack.

"Ouch! That hurt!"

She leaped back. Bena's forepaws might appear soft, but their sudden and unpredictable movements made her jump. It didn't really hurt much, but for some reason being swiped by a cat *felt* like it did.

"Why did you hit me? Am I making too much noise? Are you trying to sleep?"

But Bena's round eyes were wide open and he didn't look remotely sleepy.

"Ugh, it's fine. I'm going to read from the printouts now, so listen to me, okay?"

She gathered the backup printed pages in her hand. Just in case, she was going to practice with these, too. So long as she didn't stumble over her words, everything would be fine—

Whack, whack, whack!

"What? Why do you keep hitting me? Is my presentation that bad?"

This felt different from when Bena had pressed his paws on her parents' laps, as if stamping them with his paw pads. And it was nothing like when he'd knocked over the cans.

As Bena couldn't speak, she had no idea what he was

trying to communicate. His face was not as expressive as a person's either.

"Why does he keep on hitting me? It feels like he's telling me I'm not doing a good job . . ."

She was about to look up "what your cat is trying to tell you with his paws," when she heard a gentle knock. Her older brother poked his head through the door.

"I heard there's a cat here?"

"Yup."

Fūko gestured at Bena with her eyes. Her brother's face lit up.

"Wow, you've actually got a cat. Let me take a pic."

He took out his phone and began snapping pictures of Bena as he lounged across the bed.

"I heard you're cat-sitting for a friend. If I'd known, I wouldn't have made plans for tomorrow. Maybe I'll skip the barbecue."

Like her parents, her brother seemed thrilled to have Bena around.

And she understood why. Unless something extraordinary occurred, it was unlikely they'd ever have a cat of their own. Her parents and brother, much like her, were cautious to a fault. When it came to living things, there were no certainties. They chose to play it safe, watching other pet owners enviously and from a distance.

That was why they were all buzzing at the prospect of looking after a cat for a few days.

A cat in our home. One we can pet. It was a precious experience.

"Let me take a video. I'm going to say he's *my* cat for now."

Her brother squatted to his knees, gleefully filming Bena.

Fūko looked on, amused.

"You know I'm returning Bena soon, right?"

"That's okay. Saying I have a cat makes me seem more likable. Wait! I can show everyone the photos at the barbecue."

"So you're going after all?"

"Tomorrow's quite important. If I show this video to my work colleagues, they'll go crazy about it."

By "colleagues," he meant "female colleagues." She cringed on his behalf.

"Okay, let's lean into my whole cat-guy vibe . . ."

He brought his phone close to Bena's snout, hoping to get a close-up.

For a split second, Fūko thought a black rubber band had snapped.

That was how fast Bena had swatted the phone from her brother's hand. It bounced across the carpet several times.

Fūko and her brother froze. The room fell silent.

The only thing moving was Bena's tail. It swept back and forth as if measuring striking distance. His face was blank, but his eyes simmered with quiet anger. Seeing Bena like this, Fūko realized she had been right: when something irritated Bena, he hit hard.

"Bena doesn't like you because you keep saying he's your cat."

"What? He doesn't like me?"

Fūko's brother stretched out his arm warily to grab his phone. Fortunately, the screen was intact—no cracks, no scratches. But the momentum of that move just now—it had been too fast to dodge.

"Got it. I was wrong. Sorry, cat."

Her brother looked so dejected that Fūko felt sorry for him. Maybe if he stayed still for a bit, Bena would approach him and play.

"Just sit quietly, okay?" she told her brother.

"What? Do I have to give up on being a 'cat guy' already? I don't want to be disliked."

"Never mind that. Just sit."

She made her brother kneel on the carpet. After a few moments, Bena climbed down from her bed. Because he was slender and long, he moved as if he were flowing water. The way he circled her brother reminded her of a predator about to pounce on its prey. Her brother looked terrified, waiting for the next strike.

Bena stopped in front of him, sat down, then tapped the boy's knee with his paw. It was just a tiny tap, but her brother beamed.

"Wow, he's absolutely adorable!"

"Lucky you," replied Fūko.

The feeling was electric. There was just something so powerful about a cat—just by being there, it could fill your heart. Still grinning to himself, her brother left the room. Bena rested his chin on a cushion in the corner. His eyelids began to flutter. This time, he really did look sleepy.

Fūko's phone rang. It was Kinnosuke. To her astonishment, he said he was standing outside her house. She hurried over to look and, sure enough, there he was.

"What's going on?" Fūko asked.

"I brought you some more wet cat food. You can give them as a main meal."

Kinnosuke held out a plastic bag with several cans inside.

"You came all the way for this?"

"Well, I only gave you treats earlier. These are actual meals. If he doesn't eat the kibble, you can give him this. Or you can mix them together if you need to."

"Oh, *thank* you."

He had been concerned—whether for the cat or for her, Fūko wasn't sure. Either way, she was grateful for his kindness.

"Everyone in my family is obsessed with the cat. My dad came back early from the pachinko parlor, and my brother was so hurt when the cat snubbed him."

Kinnosuke laughed. "Cats can have that effect. Doesn't it make you want to get one?"

"Um, yeah . . ." Fūko glanced down and chuckled softly. "Maybe the opposite."

"The opposite?"

"To be honest, I'm shocked by how strong an effect it's having. I feel like getting a cat could change my life completely."

"Makes sense. You're being so responsible. Plenty of people think they can handle pets, looking only at the fun part. In reality, nothing ever goes as planned once you actually have one," Kinnosuke remarked with a grimace. "Life doesn't always go as planned, does it? How about you, Fūko? Is everything going smoothly for you?"

He was smiling, but there was melancholy in his eyes. She had noticed it earlier in the shop—he was as cheerful as he had been as a child, yet there was a shadow behind it. It wasn't just that he'd grown up; there was something careworn about him, a sense that he had given up.

"Well, for me . . ."

The answer to whether things were going well for her was "not really." Right now, at least, she had a lot of worries.

"Things aren't going exactly as I would like. I'm tackling a task at work that's outside my comfort zone, and it's making me anxious. Maybe it's because I'm so gloomy that Bena keeps swiping at me."

"Ah, the cat punch!"

"Cat punch?"

"I got it on the chin, too, remember?" said Kinnosuke, sticking his chin out.

Cat punch. That's what it was.

When he had hit out at the doctor at the clinic, it had been more like a full-on smackdown. If his claws had been out, it would have been a bloodbath—a scene from a splatter film.

"Cat punch, huh? I've heard of that, but this is my first time seeing it. It's a funny movement, isn't it? And it's pretty powerful, too."

"Cats throw them often. Suddenly, viciously, one after another. If their claws are out, it'll bring tears to your eyes."

"Can they actually break skin and make you bleed?"

"Oh, yeah, for sure." Kinnosuke scrunched up his hands into claws. "Cats will scratch you for no reason at all. The cat I used to have was super moody. I never had any idea what he was thinking."

"So there was no reason why he hit you?"

"None at all. He was just acting on a whim—just felt like it."

"I didn't know that about cats."

So, Bena is pummeling people for no reason at all!

It had felt like Bena wanted to communicate something, but there was no way Fūko could unlock the secrets of animal behavior and psychology in just one day.

Kinnosuke had been around animals all his life—you could call him a pro. And if he'd had a cat as a pet, he'd know his stuff. People often said that cats were fickle, and if Kinnosuke said it, too, it was probably true.

"Cats aren't like dogs—you can't really train them. There are a few things you can teach them, like using the litter tray and discouraging biting, but at their core they're free spirits. They only do what they want to. I envy them. We humans could never get away with it. But I guess work's been tough for you, too, right, Fūko? When I worked in Tokyo I had a lot on my mind, but even during difficult times I found moments of joy. Now all I do is process online orders—there's not much joy in that."

His tone was resigned. The bitterness in his face confirmed it. Unlike the minor problems Fūko had, it seemed Kinnosuke was dealing with a lot of regret and frustration.

When Fūko went back inside, her mother poked her head out from the living room.

"Were you talking to someone?"

"Yeah. Do you remember Kinnosuke? The son of the family that runs Takatō Dog and Cat Garden. He's teaching me lots about looking after Bena."

"Ah, that's right! You and Kinnosuke went to elementary school together, didn't you? A few years ago his father became ill and he's taken over the family business. Very impressive."

"Yes."

A former classmate who had already started taking care of his parents—she and Kinnosuke had reached that age now.

Fūko was about to go back to her room when her brother approached her.

"So, do we have the cat for the weekend?"

"Yep. I'll take him back on Monday when I get home from work."

"*Monday?*" Her brother seemed disappointed. "I have another get-together next week. Would it be wrong if I kept up the 'cat daddy' persona until then?"

So that was it: he wanted something to talk about with the girls at work. She felt a bit sorry for her brother, so eager to spin into social currency the story of a cat that his sister was only looking after for three days.

"I don't know about calling yourself a 'cat daddy' when you don't know much about cats. But if you like them, that's something, right? You could be a 'cat lover,'" suggested Fūko.

"Oh, that's better." Her brother's face brightened. "It really did lift my spirits when the cat gave me a tap just now. Good. From now on, I'm going to be a 'cat lover.'"

He seemed satisfied with this outcome. He'd probably go around proudly declaring his love for cats at every get-together from here on out.

But Fūko understood. In just one day Bena had captured the hearts of her entire family—his charm was undeniably magnetic. Sitting on the floor cross-legged in her bedroom, watching Bena sprawling confidently over the center of her bed, she felt this strongly. This was what cats were like. Instantly effective—and way too potent.

Monday morning was nothing like she'd imagined.

She'd expected to wake up miserable—she'd had difficulty falling asleep recently, and when she finally drifted off, she was racked by nightmares. She'd pictured herself trudging into work with a cloud over her head.

But to her surprise, last night she had slept well—thanks to Bena sleeping on her bed.

To be fair, all he'd done was curl up in a ball at the

foot of her futon, settling himself there while she was still in the bathroom, so Fūko had folded herself in half so as not to disturb him.

Still, the thought of a cat resting at her feet had made her smile. The room had been dark, and it wasn't as if she had been holding him in her arms. In fact, if he had been too close to her, she might have felt scared. Particularly because while she was rehearsing her presentation on Sunday, Bena had remained by her side the entire time, swiping at her frequently.

"The day is finally here, Fūko."

When Fūko got in to work, she was immediately approached by her co-worker Misaki, who had joined the company a year before Fūko and worked in the same department.

Before officially beginning their workday, everyone in the department was taking a few moments for themselves. Some were enjoying their coffee at their desks, while others were already diving into their tasks. Usually, Fūko and Misaki would chat and gossip, but recently Fūko had been using this time to practice her presentation. By now, Misaki had already listened to Fūko's presentation several times.

"I couldn't relax at all this weekend," said Misaki.

"But there's no reason for you to be nervous, Fūko. They're all pumpkins. The auditorium will be dark, so you won't be able to see the audience. You'll be fine." She nodded, as if trying to reassure herself.

When Fūko's idea had been selected for presentation a few weeks earlier, Misaki had given her friend a huge hug, praising the brilliance of her proposal. She had even pitched in to put the presentation together.

"Thanks," said Fūko as she plugged her tablet into the charger. The last thing she needed was the tablet to run out of battery halfway through her presentation. She'd even printed out the script again; her old copy was so battered it was almost comical.

Misaki tilted her head. "Hmm? You seem confident, Fūko."

"I'm not. But I'm not as nervous as I thought I'd be. At least not at the moment."

That was the truth. She had thought she might feel too nauseated to come in to work or at least have spent the morning locked in the bathroom. Yet she really didn't feel as bad as she'd feared.

Most likely it was because in the space where her nervousness and worries used to grow was now a curled-up cat. A cat had plopped itself right in the center of Fūko's heart. It wasn't that her concerns had disappeared, but Bena had clambered on top and smothered them. The mere presence of this long and slender blue-eyed cat made everything else fade into the background.

"I've done all I can. I've gone over it all so many times there's nothing more to fix, and I've rehearsed a ton. I even got smacked around by a cat."

"A cat?"

"Yeah. I've been looking after him for a friend since Saturday, and he just keeps throwing cat punches at me."

"*Really?* What kind of cat is it? Do you have a picture?"

"I do." Fūko pulled out her phone to show her. The angle wasn't great—Bena was peering upward, making his face look huge—but those bright blue eyes against his burned-brown fur made him look just like a cartoon character.

"Oh my god! He is so cute!"

Misaki's eyes sparkled as she took hold of Fūko's phone. Fūko knew that Misaki loved animals. Most of her pens and folders had cute animal designs on them.

"A Siamese, huh? I'm so jealous. I want to pet him. We used to have a cat when I was younger. Does he let you pet him?"

"Nope. If you try, he'll stop you with a cat punch."

"That sounds nice, too. I want to be punched by a cat. So he hit out at you while you practiced? That's so cute."

Misaki seemed to be truly jealous. Though it was true that Bena was cute.

But tough.

Maybe it was the dark fur around his face that made his light blue eyes seem to glow, and his tightly set mouth, which gave the impression that he was a rigorous and exacting judge of a contest who would not tolerate the slightest error.

And his actions were completely unpredictable. There was no way to tell when he'd punch, and how he modulated the speed and intensity was a mystery. Sometimes he would just give a light tap; at other times the blows would gradually become more forceful. She couldn't make any sense of it.

"Cats can be quite mercurial, you know. They will hit you for no apparent reason. That's what you call a 'hot and cold' personality type, right?" said Fūko.

"I'm not sure if cat punching indicates a 'hot and cold' personality," said Misaki. "There's always a motive behind any type of behavior. It's not always obvious what it is, which adds to the cat's charm. When a cat swipes at you, it can sting, but doesn't it make you happy? Like it chose to hit *me*."

Misaki looked spellbound. Fūko hadn't quite reached that state of mind yet, but just picturing the cat's chocolate-colored front paws brought a smile to her face.

"The paw movements are really adorable."

There's always a motive behind a cat's punches.

The instruction leaflet had said something like that, too. But the idea of cats striking without apparent reason, as Kinnosuke had mentioned, aligned better with their image. They weren't being malicious—just adorable and whimsical. For example, Bena, a Siamese, gave off the noble and strong-willed air of a capricious prince from the Middle Ages.

Fūko had to take Bena back to the clinic tonight—a thought that left her feeling a bit lonely. Thanks to Bena, her weekend had been exquisitely peaceful, and that alone made having been prescribed a cat worthwhile.

The presentation was due to begin at ten, and those taking part had been instructed to arrive at the venue thirty minutes before that. Taking a moment to compose herself in a bathroom stall, Fūko overheard people chatting by the sinks.

"We need to head to the auditorium soon. What a pain."

"Tell me about it. The higher-ups insisted we attend. It's Ms. Saito's day to shine."

"I guess they want to support her because she's the first female head of the R and D department and they want her product launch to make a big splash. But I feel sorry for the others. Do they even know that the competition's rigged?"

"I'm sure they do. I mean, look at the people who've been selected. Besides Ms. Saito, it's pretty obvious they're just slot fillers."

"That's so mean."

"But it's true! With the president and executive director backing Ms. Saito, anyone who tries to compete with her will just look like they can't read the room."

"All this tiptoeing around what's really going on sucks. There might be someone who's putting in some real effort, you know?"

"It is what it is. We're just employees. I'm going to sit in the back and take a nap."

"Me, too."

Fūko recognized their voices—they were staff from another department. But it didn't really matter who they were. The shocking news left her sitting in a daze for some time.

Rigged.

Slot fillers.

"That's so cruel," Fūko muttered without thinking.

Had she ever experienced anything so unfair? She had always believed this was a competition where co-workers supported and challenged one another to come up with great ideas. To think it was just a setup to make one person shine . . .

What a fool I am.

She felt pathetic, and angry with herself for not having paid any attention to the other participants. Why had they insisted that everyone submit entries for this particular competition? She hadn't read between the lines. No one had clued her in.

When Fūko had been selected, it was not only Misaki but also the head of the Accounting department who had been pleased for her. He'd seemed truly thrilled, saying that if Fūko's idea was chosen, it would be the first for their department.

Maybe everyone had already been vaguely aware of what was really going to happen.

And they had assumed that Fūko understood as well. Maybe she was the only person who had been fooled.

Fūko heard the door to the restroom swing open.

"Fūko, are you in here?"

"Yeah."

"Are you okay? Is it stomach problems? Some colleagues from the planning department came looking for you, saying you hadn't shown up yet."

"I see," Fūko responded quietly.

There were only ten minutes to go until the presentation. The colleagues who had been chatting a moment ago were now probably begrudgingly sitting at the back of the hall. She could envision the atmosphere in the auditorium. She had attended these presentations a few times herself and she hadn't really paid much attention either. She used to sit in the back on purpose so she could take a nap. She'd never really considered the nerves of the people presenting or the hard work they'd put in.

I don't want to go. I want to stay holed up in the bathroom.

But she wasn't so irresponsible as to abandon the

competition, even if it was rigged. Fūko reluctantly emerged from the stall. Misaki appeared rattled, taken aback by Fūko's serious expression.

"Are you not feeling well? Do you want to drop out?"

". . . no. I'm fine. I can do it."

Fūko gave an awkward smile. Now was not the time to gripe. When Fūko stood up tall, Misaki looked relieved.

"I have some good news. Apparently, the president can't make it—an urgent meeting with an important client came up at the last minute. Does that make you feel a bit more at ease?"

"I see."

In fact, she did feel a little less nervous knowing there was going to be one less bigwig in the room. Then she noticed something. She didn't feel nervous at all.

"They're pumpkins."

"What?"

"They're all pumpkins. Besides, no one pays attention to the presentations anyway. It's stupid to be nervous."

"Um, yeah, that's right." Misaki seemed surprised. "You're going to be fine. You've practiced so much for this. I honestly think your idea is going to be picked, because, frankly, I want to use the product you're pitching!"

Fūko offered a faint, ironic smile. Misaki seemed to genuinely believe that Fūko might win. Fūko resolved to stop being suspicious of her co-workers, both in her own department and in others, including the Planning department. Perhaps blaming the favored winner, Ms. Saito from R&D, was also a misjudgment.

Fūko had rehearsed so diligently for this. She'd even had Bena listen to her countless times.

Strangely, she felt lighter of heart.

"Fūko, it's almost time."

Hurried on by Misaki, Fūko left the bathroom and dashed over to the auditorium.

All day, Fūko felt unmoored.

Even after she had finished her presentation, she drifted through her work, her mind in disarray from the anxiety and the shock. The exhaustion had hit. But the thought of having to return Bena to the clinic was probably another reason she was feeling so unsettled.

As soon as the workday ended, Fūko hurried home and popped Bena into the pet carrier. Her mother, who had been playing with Bena until just moments before, looked a little disconcerted, but also relieved.

Fūko could understand how her mother felt. Sitting in the train with Bena on her lap, she, too, felt relieved that she was able to return him safely, everything having gone so smoothly. There had been no trouble with his meals or his litter box, and he was in good spirits. Even so, something heavy and dark was weighing her down.

The presentation had gone reasonably well.

It wasn't that all her colleagues had looked like pumpkins, but in the dark auditorium, with the lights dimmed, she'd hardly noticed them. When she'd stumbled over a word here or there, she'd thought to herself that it was a rigged race anyway and hadn't let it bother her. She thought her presentation had been passable, thanks to all the practice she'd put in.

Still, she couldn't shake this gloomy feeling. Ms. Saito, the head of the R&D department, had given the final presentation—a proposal for a laptop bag. It had looked like a truly polished product and was undeniably a strong contender. While not a novel idea, the bag came in a wide array of colors and patterns and had a fashionable design sure to draw attention when you pulled out your laptop in public or during business meetings. However, it wasn't inexpensive and the profit margin was slim. This wasn't the kind of idea Fūko from Accounts would have come up with. Nonetheless, she truly thought it was a lovely product, and the audience had responded very positively to Ms. Saito's presentation.

It was the difference between Ms. Saito's presentation and all the others that had made Fūko glum. Slot fillers had not even been necessary. After the presentation, Misaki and her fellow Accounting colleagues had congratulated Fūko, but it had only made her feel worse.

Sitting on the train, she could feel Bena's warmth radiating on her lap. Guilt washed over her for wasting her time feeling this way when her time with him was limited. She should be much happier. She might never again experience having a cat on her lap, even through a carrier.

She got off at Gion-Shijō Station and headed west. Unlike the day when she'd picked up Bena, the streets were teeming with tourists. To avoid Shijō Street, which was crowded, she turned north onto quieter roads. After passing Nishikikōji Street, she knew she was getting close. Three days ago, she had circled the area a few times. The sun had already set today, and the alley would be harder to spot. She pressed on, keeping a close eye so she wouldn't miss it.

Suddenly, a clinic's sign loomed into view.

SUDA ANIMAL HOSPITAL

It was an oldish, modest-looking place. Come to think of it, that weird doctor had said something about Dr. Kokoro Suda or something—that the real Dr. Kokoro's practice was around the back. So that meant the alley was behind this building.

But she hadn't expected it to be a veterinary clinic. He'd said to go there if she was hurt, but would a person really go to an animal hospital to have a wound inflicted by a cat treated?

Just as she was about to walk past Suda Animal Hospital, the door swung open and a man in a white lab coat emerged. With his messy white hair, he seemed to be a doctor who didn't care about appearances. He began watering the potted plants by the entrance.

Just one street over from Nakagyō's shopping street, you'd find yourself among houses and apartments. The houses were usually old and occupied by longtime residents. The man who had emerged from Suda Animal Hospital was the kind of person who would live there—a longtime local, through and through.

Fūko continued her journey down the street. This area was a mix of fashionable stores and old multipurpose buildings. It looked like the parade of storefronts she'd seen earlier. After circling the block once, then twice, she finally spotted the entrance to the alley. The building wasn't exactly "behind" Suda Animal Hospital, but there it was at the end of the alley.

Just as she was about to turn into the alley, her phone rang. It was Misaki. *What could she want?* Fūko adjusted the carrier in her arms so she wouldn't jostle Bena, then answered the call.

Misaki sounded animated. She eagerly filled Fūko in on everything that had happened at the office after she'd dashed out.

It seemed that some of today's presentations were going to be made again. The president, who had missed them because of a last-minute appointment, had announced that he wanted to see Ms. Saito present her proposal, as he had high hopes for it. This had created quite a stir, but what was even more surprising was that of the four other presenters, only Fūko had been selected for the reprise.

Misaki seemed genuinely happy, saying how impressed she was. It really did seem she didn't know the competition was fixed. She seemed so delighted that Fūko couldn't bring herself to tell her the truth. Feeling confused, Fūko hung up.

She stood stock-still.

One person redoing a presentation would seem unnatural, so they needed a foil. It could've been anyone. Maybe they had picked the person who mattered least.

That's so cruel. Fūko bit her lip.

To the president, everyone other than his favorites were just extras in a film. And she was nothing but a clerk in the Accounts department; he'd rarely had any cause to interact with her. Fūko could recall only a handful of times when she'd spoken directly to him. He almost certainly wouldn't have a clue who she was.

Still, there must have been some participants who had put some serious effort into their presentations. Fūko was one of them. It was the first time she had entered the competition. Until then, she had avoided it, thinking it wasn't her.

But she hadn't just phoned it in.

She had given it everything she had.

It stung like hell to be called a "slot filler."

The pet carrier felt warm in her arms. The heat emanating from Bena brought tears to her eyes. Fūko sniffed, then turned into the alley. She found the old building at the end, its entrance open, just as before.

Up to the fifth floor she went, pushing open the heavy door. The same nurse was at the reception window. She glanced at Fūko from under her lashes.

"Here to return the cat, Ms. Hatta? The doctor's waiting for you."

The nurse's dispassionate tone depressed her further. There were no waiting patients in the back, and the armchair was empty again.

When she entered the examination room, the doctor was already seated, white coat crisp, a faint smile on his lips. While his age and face were completely different from that of the doctor she'd just spotted on Fuyacho Street watering the plants, there was something similar about them, even though the only thing they had in common was the white lab coat.

"Hmm? Ms. Hatta, you look distraught." The doctor tilted his head in confusion. "Seems like the prescription wasn't strong enough. Though it looks like I prescribed the correct cat."

Spouting nonsense, the doctor moved to take Bena

out of the carrier, which Fūko had placed on his desk. Fūko froze. Had he forgotten how Bena had pummeled him the last time? If Bena's claws had been out, it would have been a scene out of a slasher movie.

"Um, are you sure that's the right thing to do? Even when Bena was at my house, he was throwing punches left and right." There was concern in Fūko's voice.

The doctor's hands, poised on the clasp of the carrier, paused for a moment, and then he burst into laughter.

"It'll be fine! I'm a doctor, so I'm used to handling cats," he said.

He popped open the carrier door and pulled Bena out. Bena happily lifted his rear in the air and gave a long, satisfying stretch.

"Good boy. Did you go over everything with a fine-tooth comb? Or did you tear all the knots out?"

Even though the doctor was stroking his back, Bena remained quiet as a lamb, showing no signs of his usual unpredictable swipes. Just as Fūko was thinking how sweet he looked, Bena whipped around and sank his teeth into the doctor's hand.

"*Whoa!*" yelped the doctor, making her jump. "I've been bitten! Chitose, this is serious! I've been bitten!"

The doctor waved his hands in a frenzy, while

Bena—the culprit—nonchalantly sprawled out on the desk, giving his limbs an extra stretch.

"Chitose! I've been bitten! Bitten! Ow!"

"Oh, be quiet!"

With this shrill reprimand, the curtains at the back flew open. The nurse walked in, her eyes narrowed in anger. The doctor stuck his hand out at her.

"Here! Look! I've been bitten."

"Let me see." The nurse frowned and glared at the doctor's outstretched hand. "It's nothing."

"But look, I'm bleeding."

The doctor held his bitten hand up. The angry crease between the nurse's brows deepened.

"It was just a little nip. You should be glad it was you and not our patient who was bitten," said the nurse. She then turned her gaze to Fūko, who was sitting there, dumbstruck. Her expression seemed sharp, as if she might be angry with Fūko, too.

"You aren't hurt, are you? When irritated, this cat sometimes lashes out with his claws or his teeth."

"N-no, I'm not hurt. But he did lash out at me quite a bit . . ."

She thought back to all the times Bena had smacked her with those chocolate-dipped paws.

So, he was irritated. Or was he enraged?

Misaki had said it, too—*there's always a motive behind a cat's punches.*

If there had been a reason for his behavior, then Fūko, who had brushed it off as moodiness, had failed in her role as his caretaker. Though it had been only a few days, maybe she'd missed some important signs.

"Do you think I irritated him? Sometimes he'd swipe at me pretty hard, but I just assumed he was in that kind of mood."

"There's always a reason," the nurse replied coolly. "It's the same with humans, isn't it? Unlike people, cats can't use words, so they use their paws. Sometimes cats use punches to communicate that they want you to play with them, or to beg for something."

"Want you to play with them . . ."

"It hurts," groaned the doctor, but the nurse ignored him.

If Bena swiped when he wished to play, then perhaps those initial gentle taps on her parents' knees had been signals of that. His adorable punches had completely won over her parents.

Maybe when he'd smacked the cans of wet food off

the table, that was him begging. It was more of a demand than a plea—one that got results.

As Fūko thought over the past few days, the nurse, her expression a little softer, said, "When a cat swipes for real, it can be a sign of aggression. But you have to prevent things from escalating to that point in the first place. Eliminate the cause before it turns into a fight."

Aggression.

The nurse's words felt like a prick to her heart. The blow to her brother had been just that. Having a phone suddenly thrust in his face, Bena had become angry. That was why he'd struck so hard. Her brother had been in the wrong. But after that, Bena had shown only kindness to him.

"It hurts." The doctor was still groaning.

"Of course, sometimes it can just be a sign of irritation or discomfort. Even humans lash out when they're annoyed."

"It hurts."

"Sometimes, when humans are on edge, the cat senses it. Reading the room—well, that was a skill cats mastered long before anyone else. I don't know why, but somewhere along the line, humans started copying them—"

"It hurts!"

"Will you be quiet?" yelled the nurse, her voice echoing through the cramped examination room. "Just stick a bandage on it or something!"

The scolded doctor pouted like a child. *What kind of relationship do they have?* They didn't seem like a typical doctor and nurse. Fūko frowned, baffled. Even Bena looked alarmed, his black pupils widening against the pale blue of his irises.

The nurse shot an irritated glare at the doctor, then turned to Fūko, two lines still etched between her brows.

"Anyway, cats also have things they need to communicate."

She pulled the surprised Bena into her arms, grabbed the carrier, and began heading toward the back of the room.

Fūko panicked.

"Wait! May I look after the cat a little bit longer?"

The nurse stopped but didn't turn around. "Did you say something?"

"Actually, it's not over yet—the company competition, I mean. It turns out that there's another round tomorrow. Please let me keep him one more day. I promise I won't do anything that'll make Bena lash out."

She meant what she said. She would no longer force Bena to keep her company while she anxiously practiced her presentation. She'd probably scowled the entire time. She'd thought she had managed to plaster a decent smile on her face, but her strained expression couldn't have been a pleasant sight for Bena.

She now understood Bena's punches.

What's with that face? That's not cute!

You look so stiff. Don't force a smile.

And why are you speaking in that voice? Anyone can tell it's fake. This is your idea, so present it naturally.

If she had to put Bena's actions into words, that was probably what he'd say.

The nurse looked over at the doctor in his chair.

"What should we do?"

The doctor was no longer sulking. He had a slight smile on his face, just like he had when Fūko had first visited the clinic.

"Well, the owner will be back from overseas tomorrow night, so, technically, today should be the last day of the prescription."

Hearing about Bena's owner made Fūko happy. In her mind, she pictured a high-flying businesswoman who traveled all over the world and lived in a stylish apartment, and Bena being beautifully looked after in a lovely home. She let her imagination run wild.

"I promise to bring him back at this time tomorrow. Really, I will."

"Okay, well, let's ask the cat. Aah, Chitose, please don't bring him close to me."

The nurse gave a snort of laughter and brought Bena over to Fūko instead.

A gâteau-au-chocolat cat. The eyes shining from his cocoa-colored face looked like fluorescent ice candies that would melt on your tongue.

Fūko gazed into the cat's eyes. "Bena, please will you stay with me a bit longer?"

Bena did not respond.

The nurse placed the carrier back on the desk.

"Will you move out of the way, Doctor? Ms. Hatta, please help me get the cat back inside."

"Of course."

Fūko opened the carrier door and helped coax Bena into it. With the three of them moving around one another in the small examination room, space was tight. The doctor remained in his chair, pressed up against the wall.

When Fūko took hold of the carrier with Bena inside

it, she felt different from when she had first come to the clinic.

"Let's go home, Bena."

Bena was going to be hers for a bit longer. Her parents and brother were probably going to be happy as well. Perhaps it felt like this when a relative's baby came to visit, then came back a second time. Of course, cats weren't babies, but they lit up the home in just the same way.

Will Bena sleep at the foot of my bed again tonight? Just thinking about it brought a smile to Fūko's face. This cat had filled her heart. She wasn't going to practice for the presentation anymore. All she had to do was present her idea in a way that felt natural to her. Having a cat around was a rare treat—it would be a shame to waste it by being preoccupied with something else.

As she pondered how she would spend her precious time with Bena, her worries about the next day's presentation faded from her mind.

Perhaps because it was the second time around, the two presenters found themselves in a smaller conference room, with only the president and a handful of senior executives watching. The projection screen was smaller, and the audience sat closer to the stage. This made it easier to observe their response.

At the moment, Ms. Saito from R&D was giving her presentation. She explained her idea confidently with crisp hand gestures. The first time around, Fūko hadn't had the bandwidth to take note of the other presenters' delivery, but listening to Ms. Saito now, she couldn't help but be impressed. She was sharp-witted and charismatic. If Fūko ever had a similar opportunity again, she'd look to Ms. Saito as a role model.

Fūko glanced over her script on the tablet. When she got to the end, an idea struck her.

That's it.

Bena.

"Ms. Hatta from Accounts, you're up. Please step forward."

Fūko stood up. She felt nervous. She couldn't speak as eloquently as Ms. Saito. But she'd practiced a lot, and if nothing else, she had given it her all.

A mock-up illustration of her proposed product was projected on the screen. It was a 150-millimeter-square sticky note, twice the size of the standard 75-millimeter ones. A cross of perforated lines scored the center.

As she introduced herself, the president's face caught her eye. He looked vaguely distracted, but he was at least listening.

"Typically, sticky notes have adhesive on the top edge. But these oversized examples—designed to be quartered after writing—have sticky backs on each piece. In meetings, ideas are often scribbled onto sticky notes, but because they're so small, the last bit of writing often becomes microscopic, or you end up slapping on a second note, which is neither efficient nor visually appealing. Incidentally, we already sell sticky notes in this larger size. I looked up the sales figures, and—"

She clicked to the next slide. A graph appeared.

"—there is very little demand for them. While they offer plenty of space to write, they can be too big and impractical to use. But if you could tear off unused sections or remove the parts with ideas you have since scrapped, it might have practical applications in meetings and team discussions."

Fūko took a glance around the room: no one was showing much interest.

Well, I expected that. She almost laughed out loud. It was unlikely that the big shots at the company would be fired up by a sticky note design proposed by an administrative staffer—assuming they were even listening. So she would share the idea that had just occurred to her.

Bena. For a few days, you became our family cat.

She proceeded to the next slide. A different mock-up appeared on the screen.

"This is the back of the sticky note. Usually, the back is blank, but with this one, I intentionally placed a small illustration in the center, where it would be divided into four sections. It's a four-leaf clover. When you tear off a piece, it's as if you're picking a leaf. I work in the Accounts department and go through a lot of office supplies. Is an illustration on the back of a sticky note strictly necessary? Of course not. But little touches like this can lift your spirits. It's just something small to make you smile at your desk. The illustration on this mock-up is a clover, but another option would be a cat."

Fūko lifted her gaze from her tablet and looked straight ahead.

She had finished reading her script. Now, it was time for her own thoughts.

"If it were me, I'd go for a Siamese cat. The center of its face would be dark brown, and the eyes would be round and pale blue. Even when split into four, each section could look cute. Since it's on the back, it could create a moment of personal joy, but if there were sticky notes featuring my favorite cat breed, I'd certainly buy them. And I'm sure I'd smile when I tore off a piece. I might even feel a bit guilty or that I needed to apologize. I think it would be lovely to experience small moments of joy while working. This concludes my presentation. Thank you very much for your time."

Fūko gave a slow bow. When she looked back up, she met the president's eyes.

"A Siamese, eh?"

"Yes." Fūko blinked in surprise.

"I used to have a Siamese, but the one I have at the moment is a mixed breed." He showed her his hands, which were covered in tiny scratches. "If we're going to use a cat as a motif, it's best to choose a Siamese or a calico—easy to recognize, visually speaking. Good work, both of you. That was thoroughly entertaining. I'll consider both presentations carefully."

As soon as he and the executives left the conference room, Ms. Saito came up to her.

"Ms. Hatta, I really like your proposal. The cat idea struck a chord with me."

"Really?"

"Yes. Whatever the outcome of this competition, let's pursue this with R and D. If we reassess the cost, I think we can turn this into a product."

Fūko was so taken aback she could only manage an awkward reply. Ms. Saito seemed serious about it, and when Fūko got back to her desk, there was already an email from her, copying her manager. Fūko was unsure how to respond, but she felt a little—no, very—vindicated.

The competition winner was going to be announced in two or three days, but Fūko already knew who it would be.

"Let's go out for a little celebration," Misaki said.

"Sure, but not today. I need to return the cat."

"Huh? Didn't you say the same thing yesterday?"

"I got another day with it, but strangely, my extra day felt like three. Cats are something else. Just having one around made our home feel totally different, like . . . how can I put it? . . . It's not just a home, it's a home *with a cat*."

"That's a very literal description . . . but I get what you mean. A home with a cat is a home with a cat."

"Exactly."

They both laughed.

It was true. For the few days that she had been taking care of Bena, the Hatta family home had been a home with a cat. A home without one and a home with one were two completely different things. It wasn't that one was better than the other—a home with a cat was simply a home with a cat.

When Fūko pushed open the heavy door to the clinic, the nurse glanced up at her from the reception window.

"Ms. Hatta, you can go in. The doctor is waiting for you," she said curtly.

Fūko walked into the examination room to see the doctor sitting at his desk, as usual.

"Good evening!"

Before Fūko could reply, the doctor raised a hand. "No need to take the cat out."

Fūko placed the carrier on the desk and sat down.

"Bena was a very good boy. He tapped a few times playfully, but that was about it. He was well-behaved the entire time."

"I see. That's good to hear. Chitose, please take the cat," he called out toward the back of the room.

The curtains parted, and the nurse entered with a cold gaze.

"Oh, you're not taking the cat out today?" asked the nurse.

"Well, his owner is on her way to pick him up. I'd feel bad if he got all scruffy."

The doctor placed his nose at the carrier door. Bena immediately struck out at the mesh. The doctor chuckled.

"Feisty, aren't you, little one? But you won't get me this time. And anyway—"

"What's wrong with getting beaten up a little?" asked the nurse. "You used to get into fights all the time back in the day. Though you did always lose."

"Back then, my opponents were just kids," replied the doctor.

His face seemed to have lost its usual glow, his smile hinting at things unspoken.

After a few moments, the nurse stepped forward to remove the carrier. Fūko's heart constricted as she watched Bena go.

Will I ever have my own cat? She couldn't imagine a future without one.

"Cats are very effective, but whether a person heals or not depends on the person themselves," said the doctor. "If being punched by a cat doesn't make you feel anything, then it's just a slight pain. You have thought things through and healed yourself. The cat has just given you a little helping paw. One day, if you end up living with a cat, you'll probably get bitten and scratched for real. Something to look forward to! Well now, I'm expecting a patient with an appointment. Take care."

The examination ended abruptly. When Fūko stepped through the door, the armchair in the waiting room outside was still empty. She didn't find the doctor as handsome or the clinic as popular as the rumor mill had suggested, but it had been on the nose about his skill.

After coming out of the alley, Fūko boarded the Keihan train and got off at Fujinomori Station. Her mother had driven her to the station on the way in, as Fūko had been carrying Bena, but Fūko decided to walk home. As she strolled down the street lined with shops, Takatō Dog and Cat Garden came into view. Kinnosuke had given her plenty of food for Bena, and she wanted to thank him. She peered in through the glass door; with the sun setting, the store lights looked soft and hazy.

Kinnosuke was at the counter in the back. He had spotted her through the window, so she went in.

"Sorry to bother you while you're working. Do you have a second?"

"Sure." Kinnosuke closed his laptop. "I just finished placing some orders. Are you on your way home from the office?"

"I just gave back the cat I've been looking after. Thanks for the canned food. He seemed to really enjoy it."

"That's good to hear. Cat food just gets better and better. Eventually, cats might end up living as long as humans."

"It would make me glad if they did."

"Really?" Kinnosuke shrugged, a hint of irony in his gesture. "Then they'll be just like humans. That defeats the purpose. Cats are cats—that's why they're in such demand, and in so many ways."

Kinnosuke's face hadn't really changed much since elementary school, when he had first invited Fūko over. He had simply grown up. Still, something had changed. She wondered what the cat Kinnosuke used to have had been like. Was that cat no longer in his heart? The day she had brought Bena to the store, what had made him hit out at Kinnosuke? What had bothered him so much?

She sensed that her childhood friend wasn't very happy—it tugged at her heartstrings.

"That cat that I was looking after," she said. "Well, it

turned out that he was swiping for a reason. I learned a lot from his smacks."

"*Really?* What did you learn?"

"Lots of things. That's why I think there must have been a reason he struck out at you. I don't know what it was, but I think you might. You're such an expert on cats."

"I do know a lot about cats, but cats are cats, for sure, and they're different from humans. They're not as complicated. But I understand where you're coming from. You're a kind person, Fūko."

"That's not what I mean . . ."

Fūko couldn't put into words what she had learned at the clinic. It was a powerful, unique, and peculiar therapy. It would be a good thing if Kinnosuke tried it out. For the moment, he still didn't understand what lay behind the cat's punch, but she couldn't imagine he was someone who could be hit and feel nothing.

"Kinnosuke, maybe . . . if something's bothering you, I know a doctor who'd listen to you, no matter how unimportant you think your problem is."

"A doctor?" Kinnosuke grimaced. "I don't really have much use for one."

"Just talking could lift your spirits. If you walk

around Tominokoji or Takoyakushi Streets in Nakagyō District, you'll find a narrow building. The clinic's on the fifth floor."

"Where is Tominokoji Street? The streets in that area are all the same. I know a Takoyakushi Street, though."

Kinnosuke was only half listening, organizing receipts as they talked. It was clear he wasn't interested.

Visiting a mental health clinic meant acknowledging your struggles. Regardless of how big or small your problem was, it was an act that required bravery. That was why you needed someone to give you a push. Sometimes, from a cat's paw. Sometimes, from the hand of a friend.

"Let me see. I think it's Fuyacho Street. There's a vet called Suda Animal Hospital, and the clinic is behind that."

"Suda Animal Hospital?"

The smile on Kinnosuke's face vanished and his brows furrowed in suspicion.

"If it's behind that hospital, it must be the Nakagyō Building. I think that's the building where someone I once knew rented a space to breed cats. They closed up shop a while ago, though."

"Oh, really? So you know the place. It's known as the

Nakagyō Kokoro Clinic for the Soul, though I've also heard it called the Kokoro Cat Clinic. It's a bit peculiar, but it's really excellent. You should check it out."

"Hmm. Sure. When I have time, I might."

Kinnosuke continued to flick through and tidy his papers. He probably thought Fūko was sticking her nose where it didn't belong.

How would he react if Fūko told him she had been prescribed a cat? She suspected that a former cat owner might be resistant to that idea, so she chose not to mention it. It was something for the doctor and Kinnosuke to decide together.

"When we were in second grade, I visited this store, didn't I? There were fish and little birds—I still remember it clearly."

"Second grade?" Kinnosuke tilted his head. "Is that right?"

"Yup. A couple of us from class came by. You invited us."

"Me? Would I have done something like that?"

Kinnosuke folded his arms and sighed, clearly having no memory of it. Suddenly, his face lit up.

"Wait, I remember now! Remember Miyagi? She was the cutest girl in our class. You guys used to be pretty close. I had this massive crush on her, and I thought that if I invited you, she might come along. Wow, I was sneaky for an elementary school kid."

Kinnosuke laughed, but Fūko couldn't share in his amusement. Seeing her expression turn serious, Kinnosuke looked at her with concern. "Fūko? Are you okay?"

Fūko forced a chuckle. "Right, you were hoping Miyagi would come. That makes sense."

That was the nature of childhood memories once adulthood arrived. It had likely just been a child's scheme. It felt bittersweet, yet compared to the farce of her company's rigged competition, it was rather endearing.

"I should get going."

"Ah, wait. We should grab a drink sometime. A nice place just opened near Fujinomori Station," said Kinnosuke, his voice tinged with embarrassment. When Fūko remained silent, he looked even more embarrassed and dropped his gaze. "It's just, you know, it's kind of fancy, and I don't really want to go by myself, but I thought I could ask you without it being weird, and I, uh, have something I wanted to talk to you about . . . or maybe I don't."

His train of thought grew increasingly incoherent. At that moment, he looked like his second-grade self.

"Sure. Let's go. Let's talk. I want to know what's going on in your life," said Fūko.

She walked out quickly before she, too, became embarrassed. Memories from elementary school were simply that—memories. How you matured into an adult was revealed through your actions. She wanted to listen to his problem seriously, no matter how small it might be, just like the doctor had done for her. If her support wasn't enough, she would suggest a visit to the Kokoro Clinic. And she would give him a good push.

Today, Fūko had overcome a weakness: her fear of presenting. She had also found a new goal: turning her idea into a product. Even if her oversized sticky note idea didn't work out, she was ready to challenge herself. She wanted to believe that the changes sparked by her encounter with the doctor would be positive.

She also came to a realization: she couldn't have a cat. They were just too cute—she wouldn't be able to handle it. She already missed Bena—she felt the heat building behind her eyes just thinking about him. That was how deeply the memory of a cat could linger.

There were lots of pictures of Bena on her brother's phone. Her parents had learned and accepted that they couldn't have a cat because it was too much work.

Fūko's next idea, and the one after that, would likely continue to be inspired by cats. Their paw pads, tails, and triangular ears. Not just imagined cats, but the irresistible charm of the real ones.

And each time, she'd think of Bena and feel that heat behind her eyes. As she walked to her home without a cat, she felt tears sliding down her cheeks.

To Cat or Not to Cat

2

To Cat or Not to Cat

"I don't want to go home," Kōtarō Dōjima muttered to the night sky.

Hayashida, his co-worker, let out a laugh. "Mr. Dōjima, your wife would be angry if she heard you saying that."

Kōtarō joined in with a chuckle, his breath thick with alcohol. His colleagues had also had a lot to drink, and only minutes before, they had been engaged in an excited yet incoherent conversation. They laughed together; they grumbled together. Tomorrow, all would be forgotten.

Still, those muttered words that had spilled out in a moment of sobriety had revealed Kōtarō's true feelings.

Kōtarō's supervisor, Abe, said to him cheerfully,

"Dōjima, it's been well over three months since we last went out drinking, hasn't it? You should be able to join us a bit more often now."

"We're finally at seven months. The baby's started to cry all night recently. My wife and I are getting barely any sleep."

"Then you should take a nap in the company car during the day," said Abe, his voice loud with drink. "And when you get home, make sure to take over caring for the baby so your wife can rest—what she needs most right now is sleep. When you're looking after a baby, you're sleep-deprived and on edge. You need to let her get some rest." Of course, he didn't actually mean that it would be okay to nap in the company car while out on rounds.

The street was packed with bars full of people in high spirits. A group of twentysomethings laughed raucously on the sidewalk. It was the same laughter, yes, but the way they let loose differed from the way salarymen like Kōtarō and his colleagues did. Hayashida and Kōtarō were in their mid-thirties. Abe was a little over forty. Even though they had been cheerful and making merry, Kōtarō just felt worn-out.

"Mr. Abe, how old are your kids again?"

"The eldest is in elementary school. The youngest is

still in kindergarten. They're only a year apart, so the house is total chaos. But it's fine. I've accepted that this is how things are going to be."

"A year apart, huh?"

Kōtarō's daughter, Tsumugi, born seven months earlier, had been emotionally and physically draining her parents over the past few months. But Abe had two kids, born one after the other. Even in his drunken state, Kōtarō felt immense respect for Abe. Some hardships could only be understood after becoming a parent.

He also wondered how much Abe was helping with the housework and childcare. He seemed to go out for drinks after work rather often—didn't his wife ever get cross? Three months ago, Kōtarō had been obliged to take a client out for drinks at short notice. Even though he'd made it home by ten, his wife, Marika, gave him a hard time about it to this day.

Tonight, he and his colleagues were celebrating having achieved their midyear sales goals. Marika had said a while back that it would be okay for Kōtarō to go, and her mother had come over to help out. Having prepared thoroughly for the evening, he hadn't felt at all guilty when they'd wrapped up at the first bar and moved on to a second.

"I don't think I'm quite at the acceptance stage yet. My wife's completely overwhelmed, and these days all I do is get yelled at," said Kōtarō.

"That's what having the first kid's always like. Everyone's in a panic. It's fine for the husband to be yelled at. At work, your manager and your clients yell at you. When you go home, your wife yells at you. What do you think, Hayashida? Doesn't that make you want to get married?" Abe joked, clearly enjoying himself.

But the single Hayashida didn't look convinced. "I wouldn't want that. Getting yelled at at work is one thing, but I don't see why I should be yelled at at home. Mr. Dōjima, don't you help your wife out?"

"I help her a ton! I do everything I can," said Kōtarō.

Still, Marika was not satisfied. Whatever he did, she complained; whatever he didn't do, she complained about that, too. Tsumugi did nothing but cry. And he went to work completely exhausted.

At least the company's sales numbers were strong—that was some consolation. His colleagues were all good people, and he had been able to take time off for Tsumugi's first shrine visit and health checkups without raising any eyebrows.

Plenty of people worked and brought up children in

far harsher circumstances. The very fact that he didn't want to go home made him feel guilty. Even when he was drunk, his mind conjured up images of a red-faced Tsumugi wailing and Marika's dark expression, the bags under her eyes.

"What do you feel like doing? Do we want to go on to somewhere else, just for a bit?" Abe made the suggestion lightly. Abe, too, was buzzed, but he wasn't quite drunk. He knew Kōtarō didn't get out much these days, and that was why he was inviting him. If Kōtarō said no, Abe would just laugh it off and let him go.

Kōtarō had promised to be home by ten. The idea that he had to leave all the fun so early depressed him. All around him thronged groups of young people—probably college students. He felt envious of their freedom.

I don't want to go home. He offered a silent apology to Marika and Tsumugi for thinking that.

"Let's go on somewhere, just for a bit . . ."

"All right! Hayashida, you have to come, too. Let's go to a hostess bar. It'll be my treat."

"Really? Great!"

Hayashida was thrilled.

I'm sorry, Marika, Kōtarō apologized silently.

—·—

"What is that?"

When Kōtarō looked up, a narrow building was blocking his path. The starry sky spread like a canopy above it. Somehow, he had ended up at a cul-de-sac. Until a moment ago, he had been walking alongside Hayashida, yet suddenly he had found himself alone, with no recollection of how he had ended up here.

The door of the building before him stood open and a dim light illuminated the hallway. He had no idea where he was.

Gotta find the subway. Kōtarō was about to step out of the alley when he heard a voice calling from above.

"Hey, you! Wait a second!"

It was a nasal, slightly high-pitched male voice. As he turned his drunken head, his vision spun. The voice called out again.

"*You!* Please come up to the fifth floor."

"Fifth floor? What for? Is there a bar there?"

A bar promoter? Kōtarō couldn't bring himself to look up at the building and just waved his hand.

"No, I really can't drink any more. Plus, I need to go home."

"Don't say that. Come up for a bit—I have some delicious catnip tea. We're the second unit from the end. Not the last one, mind."

"Catnip wine? What is that?"

Kōtarō had never heard of it. The name alone made it sound dangerously strong. He thought it over in a drunken haze. Even if he were to rush home now, he wouldn't make it back by ten. Marika was going to be angry with him anyway. At this point, what difference would a glass of catnip wine make?

"All right. Let's do this. Another drink."

Kōtarō walked into the building with a goofy grin on his face. He almost missed a step several times as he clambered up the four flights of stairs. The fifth floor opened onto a hallway lined with identical metal doors. The promoter had said they were definitely not in the last unit. His eyelids threatening to close, Kōtarō grabbed the doorknob of the second door from the end.

When the door swung open, he found himself in a bar with an odd atmosphere. It had a reception window.

A woman in white came out, and she was saying something. His head bobbing drowsily, Kōtarō decided this bar was a winner. A classy beauty like her could easily hold her own at a high-end nightclub. The hostess bar Abe had dragged him to earlier—the one run by Abe's acquaintance—had been so mediocre.

He was usually the serious type—the kind who steered clear of foolish jokes or anything edging on the inappropriate. But the alcohol had loosened him up.

"Miss, you're a beauty. You're so . . . elegant . . . like I might find you in Gion . . . and you would look great in a kimono. That's right. You're like a maiko."

"I am not a maiko. I've already debuted as a geiko." Her response was sharp, like a slap in the face.

Kōtarō suddenly realized that the person before him was a nurse. She was staring at him with displeasure.

A nurse? At a bar?

As he stood there, perplexed, the nurse said stonily, "The doctor is waiting for you inside." She gestured to a door at the other end of the room.

"Oh, um, okay."

He hurried through the door without a second thought, only now realizing there was no counter in sight. It was dawning on him that he might not be in a bar after all. *Oh no. That woman's probably just wearing a nurse costume.* This wasn't an upscale nightclub at all; he'd walked into some far dodgier place.

As he tried to turn back the way he had come, a voice

came through the door behind him. It was a high-pitched male voice.

"Please come in!"

Kōtarō was completely sober now. He gritted his teeth. *I've done it now.* How much money did he have left in his wallet?

Resigned, he opened the door and found himself in another strange space. A man in a white lab coat was seated at a desk.

"Good evening. It's your first time here, isn't it? Your name and age?"

This guy's cosplaying a doctor.

Kōtarō's worries ballooned. Marika had taken his credit card away to stop him from spending frivolously. What if he was stripped of everything he had because he couldn't pay the bill? He was regretting not going straight home to look after Tsumugi. This must be divine punishment for going out drinking.

The doctor was smiling.

"What's the matter? Your name and age, please."

Is he trying to get my personal information?

There was nothing Kōtarō could do. He folded his arms across his chest.

"Kōtarō Dōjima. I'm thirty-three."

"You went out of your way to come here, Mr. Dōjima. Please have a drink on us." The doctor turned toward the back of the room and called out, "Chitose, could you bring the catnip tea? It's for the patient, so you mustn't drink it yourself."

The curtains parted, and the woman cosplaying a nurse from earlier entered. She seemed in a terrible mood.

"I *know*! How rude."

The nurse set a teacup in front of Kōtarō and left the room. It looked like normal tea. He raised the cup to his nose and inhaled a whiff of roasted tea. It didn't seem to be alcoholic.

Kōtarō sensed a gaze on him. The doctor was staring fixedly at him, a glint in his eyes.

"Please, drink! It's delicious."

Kōtarō was certain there was something in the tea. Either that, or he was going to be charged something like 100,000 yen.

Marika, I am so sorry.

He took a sip of the catnip tea. It tasted normal. He couldn't say it was delicious, but it wasn't bad either.

"So, what brings you in today?" asked the doctor, his voice gentle.

Maybe it was because he was tipsy, or because this

place was so bizarre, but he felt a bit unsteady. Maybe whatever weird drug had been in that tea was starting to kick in.

What brought me in today? He was being held captive in a dodgy cosplay nightclub. He had a baby at home, and his wife was taking care of her on her own because he had let himself get carried away.

That was right. He was the one at fault. As a father and a husband, he should never say certain things, no matter how drunk he might be. Even if it was how he truly felt, he had to swallow it down.

He hated himself for not being able to do that.

"I don't *want* to say, 'I don't want to go home.'"

"I see." The doctor smiled. "Shall I teach you to cat? Chitose, please bring a cat."

Kōtarō was puzzled. Had he misheard something after drinking that questionable, possibly drugged tea? Had the doctor just offer to teach him to "cat"? What kind of verb was that? However, despite the doctor calling out, the curtains did not part. There was no movement at all.

"Huh. That's odd." The doctor stood up and peeked through a gap in the curtains. "Well, *well*. She drank the catnip tea and is now fast asleep. Our nurse is so mischievous."

The doctor sat back down, crossed his arms, lifted his chin, and audibly sniffed the air.

"Mmm. It smells *so* good. No, no. I'm starting to feel a little tipsy myself. I might even get my cats mixed up. Maybe we should call it a night."

Are they about to let me go? For a moment, Kōtarō was exultant, but it quickly became clear his joy was premature.

"But you came all this way. I'd feel bad if you left without having gained anything. So I'll teach you something. It's a little different from the real thing, but I'm quite good at it, too. I'm a doctor, after all. Okay, here we go."

"Huh?"

"Inhale, exhale. Inhale, exhale."

The doctor started taking loud, deep breaths. His chest expanded with each gulp, and his shoulders rose up and down. Kōtarō's eyes widened.

"Copy what I'm doing, please, Mr. Dōjima."

"What? I have to do this, too?"

"Of course! There are things you don't want to say, aren't there? Well, if you don't learn to cat, you won't be cured."

The doctor looked very serious, puffing out his chest

even more than before, his pectoral muscles protruding like a pigeon's.

"Come on! Inhale, exhale, inhale, exhale. Repeat!"

"I-inhale, exhale, inhale, exhale."

"Inhale, exhale, inhale, exhale."

"Inhale, exhale."

Maybe because he was still a bit tipsy, Kōtarō found it hard to breathe. He was trying his best to follow the doctor's instructions, but he felt like he might choke. This doctor was being far too energetic, and Kōtarō had no idea what he was supposed to be doing.

"*Okay*, here we go! Inhale, inhale, inhale. *Meow!*"

"M-meow!"

"That was great! One more time!"

The doctor's eyes gleamed with excitement. He puffed out his chest again, took a few more deep breaths, and repeated the mysterious wail over and over.

Someone help me.

Kōtarō felt tears fill his eyes. As he let out loud cries, he silently apologized to his wife and child. He thought, so what if he couldn't go out for drinks? So what if he was sleep-deprived every night or scolded unfairly? It was better to put up with all that than be forced into this sort of pantomime. Slowly, Tsumugi would grow older and life would become easier. He wasn't sure if that would be in a year, or two years, but he was determined to hang in there. After all, that was a parent's duty.

That was how people became parents.

The beaming doctor picked up the pace. "Come on, you can do this! Your meow lacks depth. Make it fuller!"

"Fuller?"

"You have to *feel* the cat. The depth of the cat and the depth of its fur."

Kōtarō didn't understand the difference between the depth of the cat and the depth of its fur, but he didn't have a chance to ask. He called out again and again, doing his best impression of the doctor. Only, instead of a cat's cry, it came out more like a battle cry.

"You're really good at this. I can't believe you're a beginner. You haven't taken lessons before, have you?"

"N-no way. Ha."

Where on earth would he have taken lessons in this? But he didn't mind the compliment.

Every time Kōtarō let out a cry, the doctor egged him on: "More! *More!*" The doctor was great at cheerleading. Encouraged, Kōtarō continued to meow.

Before he knew it, he was drenched in sweat. When he looked up at the ceiling, a smile spread naturally across his face from the exhilaration. The doctor nodded as Kōtarō caught his breath, his shoulders heaving.

"Not bad at all. But you're still far from perfect."

"Really? I tried very hard," Kōtarō retorted without thinking. He thought he'd got as close to sounding like a cat as was possible, but the doctor shook his head.

"You can't learn to cat in one or two tries. How should I put it? Cats are deep and furry. So, what would you like to do? Do you want to come in for regular treatment?"

Regular treatment? It seemed this was not a cosplay nightclub but somewhere far dodgier and more mysterious.

Still, Kōtarō was determined—he wasn't going to give up halfway. Above all, he felt as if something stagnant in his body was draining out with every drop of sweat.

This was cat. And he was learning it.

"Lessons, you say?" Hayashida raised an eyebrow.

Kōtarō, having wrapped up his sales calls and completed his daily reports and paperwork at record speed, was ready to rush out of the office as soon as the workday ended. Evidently the glow on his face had given him away. Hayashida, from the next desk over, had asked if he was heading somewhere, and Kōtarō had accidentally let it slip. Now Hayashida just looked exasperated.

"Lessons? When you have a baby at home? Won't your wife be upset?"

"Oh, if I told her, she'd be really upset—enraged."

Kōtarō laughed—genuinely, not out of self-mockery or irony. If Marika knew that he was learning cat at the Nakagyō Kokoro Clinic for the Soul, "rage" wouldn't even begin to describe it—he'd incur the wrath of god. Or maybe she'd be stunned? Completely flabbergasted?

Hayashida grinned and lowered his voice. "Are you really taking 'lessons'? Or are you doing something sleazy?" He knew full well he'd be in trouble if anyone overheard.

Kōtarō was aware that no one would understand why he'd be taking lessons after work, given his current situation. That was precisely why he hadn't breathed a word to Marika or to anyone else, and frankly, even if he had, who on earth would believe him?

"No, nothing sleazy. I'm just going for vocal training."

"Singing?"

"Well, it's . . . I guess it's a kind of singing. Vocal exercises. Great for stress relief."

"I see," said Hayashida, seemingly satisfied with this answer. "Well, if it helps with stress, then it's definitely healthier than grabbing drinks after work. When did you start these lessons?"

Kōtarō responded to Hayashida's question with nothing but a laugh and left the office. He had begun taking these classes two weeks ago, after that Friday night when he had gone out drinking with his colleagues. The cosplay nightclub he had wandered into had turned out to be the Nakagyō Kokoro Clinic for the Soul, a mental health clinic. It was a very peculiar clinic staffed by a single doctor and a nurse. Every time he visited, he saw no other patients, plus his treatments were free. He was a bit suspicious that they might try to charge him an enormous sum at the end. Still, he was hooked on how much better he felt after practicing cat.

After his first two lessons, his meow had improved considerably. He'd even learned the subtle purr. In the third lesson, he'd practiced not a meow but a hiss. He'd opened his mouth wide, bared his teeth, tented his fingers as if they were claws, and then let out a powerful "HISSSSSS." How many times had he practiced it? His jaw was sore, his cheeks were stiff, his throat was parched.

Wailing back and forth with the doctor at such close range and in such a cramped examination room made Kōtarō feel as though he were a real cat. The exercise required him to scrunch up his nose as hard as he could, and the wrinkles seemed to be still there when he returned home. That was how hard he was wailing.

Today was his fourth lesson. When he walked into the clinic, he found the nurse sitting at the reception window. She glanced up at him.

"Mr. Dōjima, please head in. The doctor is waiting for you."

She was a graceful beauty, but her demeanor was unfriendly. It seemed that, because Kōtarō had drunkenly hit on her the first time they had met, she thoroughly disliked him now.

The doctor was sitting in the examination room, a slight smile on his face.

"Ah, Mr. Dōjima. You're looking quite well. You're getting to the point where you don't have to say the things you don't want to say anymore, aren't you?"

"Yes. My wife continues to lash out at me, but I'm able to brush it off now."

"Really? That's *excellent.* Please continue to work hard."

"Absolutely!"

Kōtarō clenched his fist and braced himself.

Karaoke and belly laughs can reduce stress. Running and going to the gym can boost your mood. But this—wailing like a cat—not softly or gently but at the top of your lungs—there was nothing quite as exhilarating. Who knew this kind of therapy existed?

"Now, inhale, exhale."

"Inhale! Exhale!"

Kōtarō took a deep breath and exhaled.

"Inhale, inhale, now open wide—aaaooww!"

"Aaaooww!"

He arched his throat, jutted out his chin, and yowled as loudly as he could. His tongue nearly cramped up, and he began choking.

The doctor chuckled, watching Kōtarō collapse into a coughing fit.

"That won't do. You need to make the back of your throat vibrate more. Let your voice resonate."

"I-I see."

"You don't have to make it sound pretty. 'Aaaooww' should come from a lower register—but with the final syllable, try to express a kind of aching sadness. Aaaooww! Aaaooww!"

Wow! Kōtarō's eyes widened. The doctor continued to emit low yowls, as if he were a real cat. Not wanting to be outdone, Kōtarō strained desperately to make his throat vibrate. Even though his voice was growing hoarse and raspy, he continued to yowl.

"Aa-aa-aaow."

The doctor laughed. "Your throat is dry. You've lost your voice. My bad, Mr. Dōjima. Since you're so enthusiastic, I also got a little too fired up."

"Oh . . . really?"

He swallowed and admitted to himself that he had overdone it. His face was flushed, as if he had sprinted as fast as he could, and now he was panting. That was how loudly he had shouted. He took another deep breath and finally began to feel like himself again.

"But I've really enjoyed these lessons. Ever since I started coming to this clinic, I've found I'm naturally able to smile, even when my daughter is crying. The old me, even while I was soothing her, was close to bursting into tears myself. I found her cries painful to hear . . . even though she's my own child."

"The fact that you're able to reflect like this means you've learned enough. Come for one more lesson next week. That'll be our last cat lesson."

"*What?*" Kōtarō pitched forward in surprise. "Our last lesson? But I haven't mastered being a cat yet."

The doctor gave a chuckle.

"The goal isn't to become a cat, Mr. Dōjima. You simply learned *to* cat. Look, you've stopped saying you don't want to go home, even if that might be how you truly feel. That's because at this clinic, you've been spitting out what you've been holding in."

Kōtarō's joy suddenly vanished. He felt like he had been punched in the gut.

It was true that he had stopped saying he didn't want to go home, but Marika was still angry every day, Tsumugi kept crying, and he couldn't get a decent night's sleep. The reality was that he didn't want to go home. Nothing had changed.

He was just holding everything back.

The doctor had uncovered a truth that Kōtarō preferred to keep hidden, and it left him feeling shaken.

"I'm not . . . holding in anything."

"Ohh, is that so? Well, excuse me, then. But humans

have a habit of holding back things they want and don't want to say. It's scary because when they vomit out the stuff they've been holding in, they typically overdo it."

"Overdo it?"

"*Exactly*. Both humans and cats can be ungraceful. If they continue to hold things in, they'll continue to swell until their stomachs are ready to burst."

The doctor gave a gentle smile, but what he said had made Kōtarō feel uneasy.

Lately, the chaos at home hadn't irritated him, but that had just been because he had been releasing his stress through meows and hisses. Ultimately, he had simply replaced alcohol with cat.

What would happen if he could no longer use this method of coping with stress?

It would be out of the question for him to wail loudly at home. Marika was already at her wits' end with Tsumugi's nonstop crying. If he cried, too, she might have a nervous breakdown.

"Um, say I *am* holding things in . . ."

"Okay, let's say that." The doctor nodded.

"Now, even though I went to the trouble of learning how to meow and hiss, if I'm not able to do them anywhere other than the clinic . . ."

"Not even purrs or aaaoowws?"

"Exactly. I can't purr or aaaooww anywhere else. Does that mean I'll go back to saying I don't want to go home?"

They were having a bizarre conversation.

But Kōtarō was deadly serious. He did not want to say he didn't want to go home again. It was too irresponsible as a father.

Kōtarō had fallen silent. The doctor ignored it. He smiled brightly.

"It'll probably get worse if you keep holding it in. When it finally comes out, the explosion is usually huge. But you'll be okay—you're great at purring and chirping. Just make sure to cough it all up before you reach your limit." The doctor let out a peal of laughter.

Kōtarō had not learned how to chirp. And what did the doctor mean by "cough it all up"?

"Our patient with an appointment is about to arrive. So, take care now."

That was how the doctor ended every appointment.

It was a strange clinic, but it was also a precious place that helped him forget the problems he was having in his daily life. But after one more visit, all this was coming to an end. On top of that, this mysterious "cough it all up" was now hanging over him. It couldn't be anything good, that was for sure.

Kōtarō left the clinic in low spirits. Suddenly, the door of the neighboring unit burst open and a man flew out.

"*Aha!* I caught you red-handed!"

The thuggish-looking man was wearing a loud shirt. A thick silver chain gleamed at his wide-open collar. The man stepped toward him, forcing Kōtarō back against the wall.

"What are you talking about?"

"What am I talking about? I know you're running an unsavory business in there." The man pointed at the metal door that Kōtarō had just closed. He rattled on hysterically, "Don't try to play dumb! I've been hearing cats meowing these past few weeks. You're not allowed to keep animals in this building. This room especially has a shady history, and if you have any cats in there at all, you'll pay for it."

"Excuse me—"

"There's a bunch of people coming in and out, and there's something strange rigged to that door. It's all very suspicious. You have cats in there, don't you? Not just one or two—I've heard several cats meowing with my very own ears."

"Um, that was me, actually."

"I'm not trying to be a champion of justice or anything, but as the protector of Japan's national health, I can't turn a blind eye to the wrongdoing taking place in the unit next door."

"The cat cries—that was me," said Kōtarō apologetically, even though he was secretly smirking.

The man continued to glare threateningly at him, frowning. Typically, Kōtarō would be trembling in his boots if such a scary-looking man confronted him. But right now, he was feeling elated.

To be mistaken for an actual cat—well, I never!

"It was me that was meowing."

"Huh? What do you mean?"

Confusion swam across the man's face. He was in his mid-thirties, deeply tanned and weather-beaten. If anything, he was the one who looked shady. Now that Kōtarō thought about it, on the first night he had wandered into the clinic, the doctor had told him, "We're the second unit from the end," then added, "Not the last one, mind." It seemed like there was a bit of tension between the neighbors.

But Kōtarō couldn't blame the man. Even if it was part of the treatment, all that shouting had to be a nuisance.

And on top of that, the man mistakenly believed that there were real cats crying in the unit. Kōtarō grimaced and bowed in apology.

"Sorry for being so loud. There's a rather unusual clinic here that teaches patients to cry like cats. It's such an effective stress reliever I got carried away and must have been very loud."

"Huh?" The man frowned. "It was you crying?"

"Yes. I'm really sorry. I must have sounded like the real thing."

"This entire time, it was *you* pretending to cry like a cat?"

"Yes, these past few weeks. But there might be others who are also learning to cat. The doctor did mention something about a patient with an appointment."

"Learning to . . . cat?" The man's fierce expression turned blank. "So, there are no cats in there?"

"Not a single one."

"What the hell . . . That's impossible . . ."

The man seemed bewildered. He was mumbling to himself as he disappeared into the unit in the back.

Kōtarō chuckled to himself. The man had called himself some odd things, like a "champion of justice" and a "protector of Japan's national health." But more than anything, Kōtarō was tickled that his cries had been so good they had been mistaken for the meows of an actual cat. He had only one more cat lesson left, but if he was this close to sounding like the real thing, perhaps he had learned all he could. Kōtarō skipped down the stairs and walked out of the building.

He took the train home, getting in at eight o'clock—earlier than usual. As he reached the hallway outside his apartment, he could hear Tsumugi crying inside. When he went in, he was met with complete chaos. The mess on the floor made it clear that it had been a difficult day. A grocery bag sat abandoned by the entrance. Shoes were scattered in the hallway, as always. There was a mound of laundry in the living room, and baby food splattered the table.

Tsumugi was crying, red-faced, in her crib. She wasn't just fretting or in a bad mood: she was full-on wailing.

"Now, there, there, Tsumugi. Daddy's home."

After washing his hands, Kōtarō gently pulled Tsumugi into his arms. She was sweating from her exertions, and warm like a freshly steamed meat dumpling. Despite being held and rocked, she was crying even louder, choking on her own wails and then starting up again.

A few days ago, he wouldn't have wanted to pick up Tsumugi right after coming home from work. Even with the train ride, it was hard to switch gears after a day at the office. He was always buried in tasks at work, and even when he managed to finish everything for the day, there was always more waiting for him the next morning.

Despite having a busy day, a father always took his child into his arms as soon as he returned home. Surely that was the normal thing to do and what everyone was doing.

Now, he understood why Marika was cross with him. Kōtarō had only sluggishly and unwillingly held Tsumugi. *I'm exhausted, but here I am, caring for our child.* That was what he had been thinking, and it had shown in his attitude.

Marika emerged from the back room. Her hair was disheveled and she was dressed in sweats.

"Welcome home."

"I just got back," he replied. "Oh, I'm fine with anything for dinner."

". . . anything?"

"I'll watch Tsumugi. You take your time."

Marika repeated his words again.

". . . time for myself?"

Kōtarō walked around the living room, rocking Tsumugi in his arms. She had not stopped crying yet. Their neighbors in this building were kind. The man in the next-door unit at the clinic had rushed out after hearing a cat's cry—and a fake cat, at that.

A small chuckle escaped him. This was the first time he'd felt so calm. Meanwhile, Tsumugi's eyelids seemed to be growing heavy: she was beginning to nod off.

"You make me so cross."

When he turned to the source of the low, thorny voice, he found Marika glaring at him.

"You make me so cross. That look—'look at how much I'm putting up with for you'—really gets on my nerves."

"What . . . ?"

Kōtarō stared blankly at her. When he stopped walking, Tsumugi made a grumbling noise.

"Oh no, I'm sorry, Tsumugi." Kōtarō rocked her back and forth. Marika was looking daggers at him. He had no idea what she had meant by her criticism.

"What do you mean? I don't really feel like I'm putting up with anything."

"You do." Marika averted her eyes. "Just the other day, you were scowling the entire time you were holding

Tsumugi. And now you're suddenly all smiles. It's weird. It's obviously an effort for you."

"That's . . ."

"It's an effort for you. It's tough, I know. You don't have to put on a smile as you soothe her. It's my job to put up with things. I'm her mother, after all."

Marika looked down at the floor, tears rolling down her cheeks.

Kōtarō stood there, dumbfounded. Since their child had been born, Marika had been angry every day. And she had complained every day.

But today was the first time she had wept silently like this.

He couldn't understand why she was crying. Before today, whenever Kōtarō had held his child resentfully, she would become angry, but as soon as he had calmly picked up Tsumugi into his arms this evening, Marika had burst into tears.

You're suddenly all smiles. It's weird. It's a mother's job to put up with things?

Even without his rocking or walking around with her, Tsumugi had fallen fast asleep. Her face, which had been so red only a moment ago, had softened into a peaceful expression, and she looked almost angelic.

Thinking, *What a cutie she is*, he couldn't help but ask himself why, even though she was so sweet, he and his wife were finding it so difficult. Just looking at Tsumugi filled him with joy.

He had gone to that mental health clinic for two weeks, but he couldn't even think of any words to say to comfort his crying wife. It seemed nothing had been resolved. The cat cries he had learned hadn't solved anything.

Friday arrived.

As Kōtarō was sluggishly tidying his desk at the end of the day, Hayashida came over to him.

"Mr. Dōjima, don't you have your vocal training class today? You look really down in the dumps."

"Ah . . ."

Kōtarō forced the corners of his lips to turn up.

He was heading to his final cat lesson without having figured out what it was that Marika wanted. It was the last day of his treatment. Marika had only cried that one night. Since then, she had returned to her usual mumbling of complaints.

He thought he had been happily helping out with the

childcare that day, but having been told he wasn't, he was at a loss as to what to do. Should he have scowled, like he always did? He didn't think that was right.

Reflexively, he let out a loud sigh.

Hayashida laughed. "See, instead of taking lessons, I figured you'd want to go home early to see your baby's face."

"I guess so."

Kōtarō offered a wry smile, no longer sure of his true feelings.

It was his last lesson, but he didn't know if he was dreading going to the clinic or going home afterward.

Even if he managed to release his stress through his cat cries, if his wife was crying at home, what was the point? Maybe it was time he stopped going to the clinic. But the repeated meowing brought him so much relief. Just thinking about it brought a smile to his face. But maybe, in a marriage, it wasn't right that only one partner got that relief.

"But that's a bit . . . I don't know." The words dropped out of Kōtarō's mouth, and he laughed at himself.

Hayashida tilted his head.

"What's wrong?"

"It's just that I don't want to go home after all."

"*What?*" Hayashida drew back. "Don't say that. You're scaring me."

"I'm going to be honest—here's the truth: My wife is so exhausted that she's no longer making any sense, and my kid won't stop crying. I have no idea what I'm supposed to do. But I have to put up with it all—I'm a dad now. Both my wife and I, as parents, have to put up with everything."

That's right. Kōtarō bit his lip and nodded. *I didn't put up with things well enough. That's why Marika was crying.*

Hayashida was looking at him with concern in his eyes, but Kōtarō didn't mind. Hayashida didn't understand because he was still single.

It was a time of endurance for the sake of their child. It was a time of perseverance.

"That's impossible. It's not a level of stress you can 'put up with.'" Abe had suddenly appeared between the two men. He was laughing through his nose. "Dōjima, your kid's still only six months old, right?"

"Seven," said Kōtarō.

"What's the point of you worrying about this so much now?" asked Abe. "It's only going to get harder. At our house, both my wife and I are still running around every day."

"You have two children a year apart, so I can only imagine how tough that is. I have just one kid, and my wife stays home, so I consider myself lucky. Still, things can get pretty chaotic sometimes. Some days, my wife doesn't make dinner, even when I tell her anything'll do."

Hayashida raised an eyebrow. "She doesn't make dinner? You come home tired, and there's no meal waiting for you—that's rough."

"Right?" said Kōtarō, cheered up a little by Hayashida's sympathy.

But Abe let out a sigh. "Dōjima, you've stepped on a land mine. 'Anything'll do' is one of the things you should never, ever say."

"What? Why not?" Kōtarō and Hayashida asked in unison.

"Well, if anything was *really* fine, then you should make dinner yourself. You can get takeout, or eat out. The last thing your wife wants to be worrying about is her husband's dinner. When we had our first kid, my wife often snapped at me, too—'When I've got my hands full looking after our child, a grown man shouldn't be demanding a meal!'"

Kōtarō was alarmed. There were too many instances that came to mind—instances where he'd thought he was being considerate, but in fact he was not lightening Marika's load at all.

"You don't have to tolerate everything. When your kids are still young, you might have to do some things differently, but tough times are tough for everyone, including adults. You and your wife should cry with your kid. In my family, we reached a point where we couldn't handle it anymore, and I genuinely cried—my wife and I, we both bawled at the top of our lungs."

"Sounds like a nuisance to your neighbors." Hayashida frowned. "Enough to make an adult cry, huh?"

"The kids already make so much noise that no one can tell the difference if there's a little bit of adult crying mixed in. And our family's only growing."

"*What?*" Kōtarō and Hayashida shouted at the same time.

Abe was smirking.

"No, I don't mean a third kid! On Saturday, we're going to a cat adoption fair. Both my wife and I love cats, and we've wanted to get one for a while."

"A cat . . ." muttered Kōtarō. He almost let out a meow, but he gulped it down.

"An adoption fair?"

"Yeah. A lot of places won't let you adopt a rescue if you have small kids. But Kyoto's City Cat Rescue Center allows adoptions even if you have little kids, depending on your situation. One of the kids from my youngest's kindergarten said their family adopted a cat from there, so we thought we'd check it out."

"What's the difference between rescue cats and stray cats?" asked Hayashida.

"Rescue cats are stray cats that have been taken in by the facility, though there are other situations cats are rescued from," Abe answered. "Kittens can be a handful, so we thought an adult cat might suit us better, and in that case, we thought we might adopt a rescue. We might not find a cat we connect with, but I'm still looking forward to visiting the center."

Abe was grinning ear to ear.

Wow. Kōtarō was impressed. "You have two kids, and you're going to get a cat. That's incredible."

"More like incredibly chaotic. But it's fine. We'll add a cat to the frenzy. What if you tried to turn things upside down as well? Your neighbors are probably just starting to get used to your kid's crying. They probably won't complain if you added a cat to it."

"What?"

Kōtarō was taken aback. He never imagined that he'd be advised to get a cat.

A cat?

Kōtarō blinked repeatedly. Bringing a cat into his already-hectic daily routine wasn't something he had considered, even though for the past two weeks he had been soothed by meowing as if he were one himself.

Adopt a cat.

Was that even possible?

Suddenly, an image of a cat appeared in his mind, but it wasn't a real one. It was a hazy impression of a cat from a picture he had seen. He couldn't remember ever seeing a real cat up close. Maybe he had, but the memory wasn't something he'd held on to.

He left the office with an odd, uneasy feeling in his chest.

When he opened the door to the Nakagyō Kokoro Clinic for the Soul, the nurse at the reception window glanced up at him briefly.

"Today's the last day of your treatment, Mr. Dōjima. The doctor is waiting for you."

She really was a classic beauty you might see around Gion, the entertainment district of Kyoto, but her attitude, as always, was chilly. It seemed she was still holding a grudge from their first meeting. He was thinking, *She could at least give me a smile on my last day*, when she shot him a sharp glare.

"Can I help you with something?"

"N-no, nothing."

He hastily entered the examination room, where he found the doctor—he was smiling faintly—waiting for him.

"It's your final appointment today. Today, I'm going to teach you the very special *mraaoow*. Please put up with the things that are challenging you, and hold back your true feelings. Even if you don't want to go home, don't say that out loud—just cry it out. Now, are you ready? Mraaoow is a long cry, so please take a deep breath to prepare."

"Um," interrupted Kōtarō.

The doctor tilted his head. "Yes? Do you have any questions?"

"I, um . . ."

Kōtarō clenched his fists on his lap. *The very special mraaoow. I bet that'll feel good.*

But he'd still be putting up with the challenging things, holding back his true feelings and leaving things unsaid.

None of that felt right at all. A smile faked like that was no smile at all.

"I'm thinking about not holding things back anymore. Even if I let off some steam here, my true feelings end up slipping out anyway. The truth is, I don't want to go home. I love my child, and I do want to help out. I want my wife to be in a good mood, and I don't like it when she scolds me. This is how I truly feel—and it can't be expressed with a *meow* or a *hiss*."

He was being selfish and irresponsible.

But it felt much more appropriate than meowing or hissing. It was pathetic, but this was how he really felt.

"Oho." The doctor sounded impressed. He smiled brightly. "That's bold. Just leaving it out in the open, not even bothering to cover it up with sand. What a wild person you are."

"Leaving it out in the open . . . with *sand*? Huh?"

"But when you leave it out in the open, the truth can smell quite strongly. Your wife and child might find it smelly. The smelly truth . . . All right, I'm going to teach you an easy meow that you can do at home so that doesn't happen. Not to worry—you won't need to raise your voice. What you need to do, Mr. Dōjima, is a silent meow."

"A what?" Kōtarō frowned. "Can you repeat that?"

"A silent meow."

The doctor looked deadly serious.

"Meowing is just the beginning. How your true feelings will evolve depends entirely on you. Maybe it'll continue to stink, or you might develop a desire to return home and help out in new ways. Until you genuinely feel that deep down, let's cry wholeheartedly—but silently."

That makes no sense at all.

But there was not a single thing at this clinic that made any sense. Since the night he had drunkenly wandered in, it felt like he had been living in a hazy dream, something fluffy he had seen somewhere. A blurry image floated in his mind, but the image remained unfocused.

"All right. I'll do it—the silent meow. Please teach me how."

Seeing that Kōtarō's expression had become serious, the doctor grinned back like a mischievous child.

Tonight, again, Tsumugi's cries leaked into the hallway of the apartment.

When he went inside, as always, things were a mess. The dishes from breakfast were still on the dining table. He almost tripped over the toys on the floor.

Then he laughed. It seemed Tsumugi was going to be a handful for a little while longer. Just as Abe had said, it wasn't a level of stress you could "put up with."

He picked her up from her crib and began walking around the living room with her. Even as he rocked her gently, she continued to cry with her whole tiny body. It was similar to the silent meow Kōtarō had just learned. Mouth open wide, teeth bared, body shaking. A full-hearted, voiceless cry that turned her face crimson.

Ah, that's what Tsumugi is doing. Every day.

Working all day was tiring. Caring for a child all day was challenging. But perhaps the one who was most tired and most challenged was the baby who was crying with all her might.

"Tsumugi, you're so talented. Daddy was exhausted after three tries."

Bouncing her gently in his arms, he brought the bawling Tsumugi's head to his face and took a sniff. Her sweaty smell made him smile.

"You're back."

Marika stood there, her expression dark. Perhaps she'd just woken up, but her eyes were not fully open.

"I'm sorry, I haven't made dinner." Tears begin to roll down her cheek.

Seeing Marika like this, Kōtarō realized that it was his wife who had been putting up with a lot. He wished he had cried with her earlier. Now he knew the grown-up way to cry.

"I learned something helpful from a colleague at work today. He said we don't have to put up with anything, and we can just cry together. So let's cry with Tsumugi. I'll do it, too."

Kōtarō laid Tsumugi down in her crib. She threw her head back and made a big fuss.

A bright red face, messy with drool and tears. Crying this loudly must feel good.

If you were going to do it, do it with this level of passion.

Kōtarō curled his fingers into claws and took a deep breath.

Then, harnessing all his might, he let out a voiceless scream. It was a full body-and-soul silent meow.

He leaned into Tsumugi's head, inhaled, then let out another cry.

A lungful of air. These were the true feelings he could express right now. It was hard for adults. It was hard for fathers. It was also hard for mothers. So they would stop tolerating things and cry loudly. After he repeated this action a few times, Tsumugi opened her eyes wide and started sucking her thumb.

Kōtarō laughed. "Look, when I cried, she stopped crying."

He turned around to see Marika standing there, open-mouthed.

"What are you doing?" she asked.

"Silent meowing. You try it, too."

He meowed voicelessly. Marika shook her head.

"No way. What is that?"

"Pretend to cry like a cat. When you want to cry, instead of holding it back, it's better to just let it out. But if all three of us cry out loud, we'd be a nuisance to the neighbors. So he taught me to cry voicelessly."

"Your colleague taught you this?" Marika looked incredulous.

He'd learned it at a peculiar clinic either on Rokkaku or Takoyakushi Street.

He chose not to share that. If his wife found out he had unknowingly been drawn into a mental health clinic, it would make her worry more. And it wasn't as if he had received any real medical treatment; he had just been taught how to cat.

"Now, you try it, too, Marika."

"No way. That's so weird."

"Meow! Oops, I'm not supposed to actually say it out loud." Kōtarō, carried away, had let out a full-throated meow.

Marika let out a chuckle.

"Stop it! You're acting like a weirdo!"

"It's fine to be a weirdo at home. Daddy's not going to hold it in anymore! I'm going to purr and aaaooww as well."

"What are you talking about?" Marika burst into laughter. "That's ridiculous. You're too tired. You've lost it."

"It's okay if it's ridiculous. Come on, Marika. Meow! Purr! Chirp!"

"Stop it!" Marika was doubled over with laughter.

Tsumugi lay face up in the crib, her arms in the air. She, too, was chuckling.

Kōtarō hissed and aaaoowwed for them. He was no longer doing it silently, but if it would make them laugh, it didn't matter. All the cat cries he had learned at that clinic had come in handy.

It was a fantastic clinic. A wonderful clinic. He was glad he had gone. He was glad he had found it.

As he meowed and laughed, he felt the heat build behind his eyes.

As they walked down Takoyakushi Street, searching for a suitable izakaya pub, Hayashida turned to him.

"Is it okay for you to join us, Mr. Dōjima?"

"Yeah. My wife's given me permission to go out once a month."

There was no special occasion for their gathering—they were simply grabbing a drink on their way home on a Friday—but still, Kōtarō was so happy he had a bounce in his step. The last time he had gone out for drinks, he had drunkenly stumbled into a clinic. Now he was walking in the opposite direction.

"Once a month, huh?" said Hayashida, releasing a sigh into the night sky. "Getting my wife's permission to grab drinks on my way home—that's unthinkable for me, at least right now."

"And let me tell you, to get that permission, I have to do housework from morning till night tomorrow," said Kōtarō.

"What? Cooking meals, too?"

"Of course. And laundry, sweeping, grocery shopping," declared Kōtarō. He had said all this very righteously, but to be honest, he wasn't sure if he'd be able to get up in the morning.

But lately, Marika's mood had improved. Since the night they had burst into laughter over the silent meows, something had cracked open for them. They had expressed their intense emotions with cat cries, and in this way they were gradually able to laugh about them.

Abe joined in on the conversation.

"As if you should be bragging. Acting like you're doing something special will infuriate your wife. It doesn't matter if it's the weekend or whether you went out the night before. Helping out with the housework is a given. You have to help out every day."

"Says the guy who's always out drinking. Are you really helping out every day?"

Kōtarō was half exasperated. Abe went out constantly. If he still managed to help out at home, it would be really impressive.

"Of course. I drink, I work, and I help out at home. That's why our home is always a mess," said Abe, breaking out into loud laughter.

Abe hadn't even had a drink yet, but he was already

in high spirits. Kōtarō wasn't sure how much of it was true. If Kōtarō were to make housework and childcare a part of his everyday life, it would require more patience and effort from him. But when he struggled, he could get help from the cat cries. A silent meow and an occasional full-throated cry brought smiles to the moments he spent with his daughter.

Then he remembered Abe's plan to adopt a cat.

"Mr. Abe, you said you were going to a cat rescue center. What happened?"

"I was wondering about that, too," said Hayashida.

"Ah, yeah. My family and I went to the adoption fair. The rescue center was really big, and there were a ton of people there."

"So, did you get a cat?" Hayashida seemed curious.

Abe gave a rare, awkward smile.

"So, you see, we're on this trial thing—we've had them for about ten days. Two of them."

Kōtarō dropped his jaw in shock.

"Two? You decided to get two cats right off the bat?!"

"They belonged to a young man who lived alone, but he fell ill and could no longer look after them. The only condition was that they were not separated. I wasn't sure about taking in two cats, but my kid insisted.

However"—Abe shrugged—"both cats were on edge and kept hissing at my kid. So we figured it wasn't going to work out and took them back to the rescue center."

"*What . . . ?*" Kōtarō's voice caught in his throat.

He didn't know the rules of the rescue center. He assumed Abe had acted in accordance with them, but he had some misgivings nonetheless. But when he looked at Abe, Abe was smiling.

"After we returned the cats, we felt unsettled, like we'd made a mistake. What was going to happen to them? I started wondering if they'd ever get adopted. Once you take them in, they're no longer strangers to you, you know? My wife was saying the same thing, so we ended up going back to the rescue center last week. If they weren't there anymore, we figured that would be fate, but there they were! And now we're in a trial period with them again."

Kōtarō and Hayashida exchanged looks. Abe was grinning.

"This volunteer lady really laid into me—something about imagining how it feels to be rejected twice. She had a point, but it also takes courage to say no, and going back to the center wasn't an easy decision. Since we'd already returned the cats once, we had to consider things more carefully. Anyway, that's what happened. Now I've got two kids tearing around the house and two cats that do nothing but hiss." Abe let out a small laugh.

Hayashida looked appalled.

"That sounds super challenging."

"It is. Very. But things were challenging before, so it's okay to add a little more to it. Right, Dōjima?"

Kōtarō nodded.

"You're right."

"Exactly. It's going to work out. Our house is always a mess anyway. Doesn't it make you want to get married, Hayashida?"

"Hmm." Hayashida made an odd, noncommittal sound. "I'm not really interested in getting married, but I was interested in getting a cat. It didn't occur to me that you might not be able to care for it if you get sick. If you live alone, I guess that kind of thing can happen."

"Being aware of it can help you prepare, right? So just go ahead and give it a shot with a bam!"

"What do you mean by 'with a bam'?"

As Kōtarō listened in, he reflected, *There are all sorts of ways people meet—everyone has their own circumstances and mindsets. You can't control things like timing or fate.*

Right now, both Kōtarō and Marika had their hands full with Tsumugi and had no bandwidth to focus on anything else. But because they frequently went into meowing episodes, sometimes it truly felt like there really was a cat around. He had never really even touched a cat, but he felt the presence of one.

Now he found himself watching cat videos during his free time. Hearing how real cats meowed, he'd realized that the doctor was actually quite good at it. His voice and gestures were exactly like those of a real cat. He must own a cat himself and care for it so deeply he had adopted its patterns of behavior. Otherwise, there was no way he could meow that well. For Kōtarō to get that good, he'd need to practice even more. He needed to meow more often at Tsumugi and make her smile.

And one day, he really would consider it—the idea of getting a real cat.

He hoped Abe's cats would settle in with his family. For the time being, that was where Kōtarō stood on cats.

Akira Shiina, president of the Japan National Health and Safety Association, had his ears pressed to the wall in the unit next door. Recently, whenever there was a lull in his work, he would strain his ears for any sounds from his neighbor.

But the only things he could hear were the low, mechanical hum of appliances and the closing and opening of the door downstairs. There were no suspicious noises.

Unconsciously, he stroked the magnetic necklace hanging from his neck. Maybe the suspicious thing was sensing its magnetic powers and hiding.

The intercom rang, and in came the cleaning woman. In the Nakagyō Building, weekly floor cleaning was included in the rent. It wasn't anything substantial. The floor was wiped and the trash was taken out. The service used to be optional, but after the illegal breeding incident, it had apparently become mandatory for all tenants.

It was always the same middle-aged woman who cleaned. They were well acquainted and had got used to seeing each other. The vacuuming was always noisy, so Shiina decided to go out for a while.

"Auntie, I'm off to grab some food. Just do your thing, yeah? You can leave everything on the desk as it is."

"Okay. I'll do the windows today, then."

The cleaning woman opened the windows at the front of the building.

A pale blue, cloudy sky lay beyond them. It was the first time in a long time he had seen the sky. Only the unit situated right at the back had a window in this position. Right below it lay Fuyacho Street. It wasn't particularly scenic, and as he was all the way up on the fifth floor, the window usually remained shut.

There were also a couple of larger windows on the north side of the building. Since the building opposite was lower, plenty of sunlight streamed in. Nevertheless, he rarely opened the window. Below it was a metal platform for the air conditioner unit—barely wide enough to stand on—that was rusty and falling apart. A potted plant, left behind by the previous tenant, sat abandoned in the corner. The platform was so narrow even a thief couldn't negotiate it.

As Shiina was about to leave, he suddenly thought to ask the cleaning woman something.

"There's no one in the unit next door, right?"

"It's completely empty. Even when someone moves in, they tend to leave quickly."

"Thought so . . ."

He had checked that it was vacant several times. But just the other day, he had spotted an office-worker type coming and going. And the man had even claimed he was practicing wailing like a cat.

Maybe Ioka, the owner of the building, was secretly running a cosplay club. Ioka was wealthy and known for indulging himself extravagantly in the teahouses and restaurants in Gion. In the past, he'd even purchased Shiina's highest-grade magnetic necklace. If his sense that there were cats around turned out to be wrong, he'd feel extra foolish for having trembled over what he'd imagined was something sinister.

Feeling irritated, he stopped in front of the door to ask the cleaning woman another question.

"Have you heard anything on this floor—no, this building—that could be the sound of cats meowing?"

"Cats? No, not a thing. But I know there's a vet just behind the building."

It seemed she was eager to begin the task of cleaning. She kept her answers short and turned on the vacuum cleaner. But a moment later, she switched it off.

"Oh, wait. I might have seen some cat fur."

"Cat fur?" Shiina froze in his tracks.

The cleaning woman nodded. "Some sort of animal fur, hardened into a lump in the corner. It wasn't dust, and I wondered what it could be, but it was probably just a bit of black fur."

"Wh-where did you see that?" he asked.

"Here." The cleaning woman pointed toward her feet. "It was floating on the floor in this room. Maybe the wind blew it in?"

Then, she turned on the vacuum.

Shiina stood paralyzed in shock.

Tangerine

3

Tangerine

Orié Onodera got off the train at the Kyoto Shiyakusho Mae stop, a station that was connected to the city hall. Its underground shopping mall offered everything locals might need—bookstores, grocery shops, and stalls selling odds and ends. It wasn't glamorous. Just a practical place for people to do their shopping.

Down in the underground plaza, an event was taking place. Children's drawings were on display, and a handful of stalls were offering homemade sweets and accessories.

At one of the stalls, Orié's friend was selling her crochet and patchwork creations. Orié stepped inside the booth and took a seat beside her friend, who was wearing a skirt stitched together from bold, mismatched fabrics;

complementing this look, Orié's hair was a vivid shade of pink. They looked eccentric, certainly, but both women took their work very seriously.

"How is it going?" Orié asked her friend, who had been manning the booth since morning.

Her friend smiled wryly.

"Not great. No one's stopping to look, let alone picking anything up to buy. I was really expecting more."

Her friend looked crestfallen, but Orié responded with a cheerful smile. "Can't be helped. Over there, that's the main attraction today."

She turned her gaze toward the stage in the middle of the plaza. A junior high school brass band was setting up. The turnout to watch them was pretty good. The folding chairs in front of the stage were mostly filled, and families were bustling around the elementary school kids' drawings. It was, after all, an event to celebrate the students' work, so the stalls were more of a side attraction.

Even so, it was disheartening when the work you'd poured your heart and soul into didn't catch anyone's eye. As a fellow creator, Orié understood her friend's disappointment.

"Go and have some lunch, and take your time. I'll

look after the stall. If a long line forms and it's more than I can handle, I'll call you."

"Ha! That's not going to happen, but if it does, I'll come running back."

Orié took out her sign and business cards from her bag and positioned them at the end of the long table. On occasion, Orié got paid; today, she was working for free. In exchange, she was allowed to display her own brand of goods. Orié was an illustrator specializing in portraiture. Her charmingly stylized portraits varied in price depending on the request. For quick on-the-spot work, she used colored pencils, but for online commissions she worked in watercolor and digital media. When running her own booth, she also sold merchandise featuring original characters she'd created. Today, she was supporting her friend's stall, so she was going to keep it simple, with quick portraits.

The plaza was busy, but no one was stopping at their stall. However, she was used to this by now. At craft fairs and flea markets, only a few stalls attracted customers, while most were overlooked. Her friend's patchwork was exquisite, but because of the cost of material and labor, it was priced higher than mass-produced alternatives. It seldom sold. And after subtracting the admission fee and other expenses, she suspected her friend was running at a loss.

Orié observed the junior high school band's performance from the booth. They missed the odd note, but their enthusiasm came through. She couldn't help smiling as she swayed to the rhythm. There was joy in being absorbed in something.

Orié was already thirty, an age when society expected her to start settling down. But she'd become what she dreamed of in junior high: an illustrator. She was content, even if she couldn't make a full-time living from it.

"Excuse me."

She had been so focused on the performance she hadn't noticed the people standing in front of the stall. Before her were two women in kimonos, their hair pulled back in a traditional Japanese style. One was young—perhaps in her early twenties. She wore no white makeup, but the distinctive Shimada topknot hairstyle with its raised bangs and sides framing the face marked her as a real geisha. Her cheery pink kimono looked like it was for everyday wear.

The other woman appeared to be in her fifties, perhaps older. She seemed like the proprietress of an okiya, a geisha lodging house.

"If I showed you some photographs, could you work from them?" asked the younger woman with the Shimada coiffure, her gaze fixed on the panel Orié had put up on the table.

Visitors from outside Kyoto often believed geishas could be found all over the city, but in reality, they were a rare sight.

Orié smiled calmly, but her heart was pounding. "For a portrait on shikishi paper? Yes, and I can work from photos on your phone as well."

"How long will it take?"

"Around twenty minutes. The more subjects in a picture, the longer it will be."

"Mother, we have some time until the dinner party. Can we have a portrait drawn?" the woman with the Shimada bun asked sweetly.

The older woman smiled in amused exasperation.

"You really are something. No matter how old you get, you're still like a child. Fine. Go ahead."

"Thank you. Then, a portrait of Mother and me, please."

"Me, too?" The older woman's eyes widened. "I'll pass. Just have her draw you, Yuriha."

"Oh, come on. Let's have her draw us together. Miss, can you draw Mother, me, and oh, this little one?"

Yuriha held out her phone. Instead of a person, the screen showed a light brown cat. Its face was oval, and it had small, folded ears pressed close to its head. Its shape could almost be described as a catlike ohagi sweet rice cake.

The overwhelming cuteness of the cat made Orié smile. She often received commissions for portraits with pets, or just the pets themselves, mostly cats and dogs, although in the past clients had also asked her to draw horses and snakes. She could depict a wide variety of animals.

"Isn't he cute? His name is Mimita. He's a Scottish fold, and his ears are folded down flat, like, *splat*. It almost looks like he's wearing a ribbon, but those are actually his ears."

Yuriha scrolled through the photos on her phone. One image showed a geisha holding the cat in her arms, giving Orié an idea of the cat's actual size. But if she drew the cat to scale beside a human, it would appear too small. As Orié studied the pictures, she started visualizing the image in her mind. She planned to trisect the shikishi and draw the two women's and the cat's faces proportionally. The cat's face was roughly an oval. She aimed to echo the roundness in the two women's faces.

She seated Yuriha and the proprietress in matching folding chairs, carefully observing them from the front. As for the cat's picture, she had transferred the image Yuriha had chosen onto her tablet. Drawing pets was harder than drawing humans. Owners always spotted quirks that no artist could catch at first glance.

That was why the details mattered. The touch of white fur and the spotted markings. She also tried to capture the pets' colors faithfully. She always exaggerated the lift at the corners of their mouths to give the appearance of a smile. Even when they were baring their teeth in the photo, she never drew them exactly as they were. Someone like Orié might see such an expression as aggressive, but to the owner, even when their pet looked fierce, they found it endearing.

While Orié drew, Yuriha and the proprietress chatted.

"Mother, I want to dye my hair pink like this lady's."

"What are you saying? If a geisha from Gion had pink hair, it would alarm the customers."

"But I'd wear a wig over it. Even if my real hair were pink, nobody would know, right?"

"In that case, why not choose any color you like for your everyday wig? As long as you don't wear it to dinner events, your everyday wig could be whatever color you want."

"Oh, that's true. With a wig, I could choose any color. That's genius, Mother."

Beyond their chatter in their charming Kyoto dialect, Orié could hear the sound of the brass band. *A lovely geisha and a kind okiya proprietress.* Her pencil glided so smoothly she almost wanted to draw musical notes.

Yuriha's kimono was bright pink, while the proprietress's was yellow-green chartreuse. She brightened the colors beyond their natural hues to add vibrancy. She also warmed Mimita's fur with a touch of yellow. His fur looked glossy, accentuating his charm. To make his small, folded ears look more like ribbons, she made them taper to a point. They had requested that their names be added to the picture, so Orié wrote "Shizue," "Yuriha," and "Mimita" in rounded letters.

"Does this work?" asked Orié.

"Wow, Mimita looks so cute!"

"Oh my, this is impossible. Don't I look too young?"

Yuriha and the proprietress discussed the illustration excitedly.

Orié felt all eyes on her as she sketched. Two geishas naturally attracted attention, giving the impression that her booth was popular.

An idea occurred to Orié.

"Mimita came out looking really adorable. Would you mind if I posted this portrait on social media? I'll make sure to hide your names."

Yuriha smiled. "We don't mind at all! You don't have to hide the names. Isn't Mimita a cute name? Not that I named him or anything."

She was gazing at the portrait as if her beloved cat were right there in front of her. It was probably the same way she looked at the cat itself. People looked at their pets and children with so much love. When this was properly captured, even a simple portrait could seem to smile back at the viewer. In the portrait Yuriha had sparkling eyes, and Orié thought she had done a good job, if she said so herself.

She offered her business card in the hope that it might lead to more commissions. Yuriha accepted it with a smile.

"Are you always here, Ms. Pink Hair?"

"No, I'm not. I'm just working at this booth for this event. Usually, I accept orders through the contact info on that card, and also at the café where I work part-time. If it interests you, please visit my website—I post my schedule there. I'll put up Mimita's portrait there as well."

"Thank you. I look forward to checking it out."

Yuriha seemed delighted. Such a charming geisha must surely be popular. Even though Orié lived in Kyoto, like most residents there, she had no connection to the geisha district. But meeting people like this expanded her network, and sometimes it could lead to unexpected job opportunities.

After the two left the booth, most of the onlookers also disappeared, but a few people came over to look at the wares. Just as Orié finished processing a customer's purchase, her friend came back.

"Wait, did you make a sale?"

"I sold a cushion cover and a set of crocheted black-and-white rabbits."

"Amazing! Thanks."

Orié's friend was delighted. As a temporary shop assistant for her friend, Orié was relieved as well. With her friend back at the booth. Orié left. She took the subway and got off at Higashiyama Station.

Back aboveground, she walked a little way until a gigantic Shinto shrine archway—wide enough for several buses to pass through it—at the end of Jingu-michi Street appeared in view. Beyond its vibrant vermilion was Heian Shrine, with its verdant tiled roof.

The neighborhood was home to many large art museums, and Orié decided to go into a nearby gallery. It was a small place, rented by the hour, and there were no visitors. Right by the entrance, in a spot that immediately drew your attention, hung a landscape painting of a hazy green Mount Miyama. It was a watercolor the size of a large poster, and the label next to it read WINNER OF THE HIGASHIYAMA WARD HOMETOWN GRAND PRIZE.

It was a highly atmospheric piece that appealed to Orié's taste, and she really thought it deserved the accolade.

"Orié!" someone called out to her.

She turned, and there was Mitsu Asakura. She'd expected to see her here.

"Mitsu!"

"Thank you so much for coming! I'm so happy to see you."

Joy shone from Mitsu's smiling face. They had been classmates at art school and had both majored in painting. It had been five or six years since they had last seen each other, but Mitsu still had the same earnest charm she'd had at college.

"Your hair color is so cute, Orié. You're still so chic."

Orié laughed. "I'm already thirty—it's like, when am I going to settle down? You haven't changed at all. Thank you for the invitation. I'm impressed."

"Not at all. I hesitated to tell you, since it's not a major prize or anything," said Mitsu. "But I figured it might only happen once in a lifetime, so I thought I'd let you know."

"'Not major'! Hardly. It's wonderful."

Orié honestly believed what she said.

She surveyed Mitsu's landscape straight on. It was a painting of mountains. The rich gradations of green were beautiful. It wasn't groundbreaking, but it was a classic, traditional piece with a certain elegance.

Orié had been thrilled to receive the card from Mitsu announcing that she had won the prize. After graduation, Mitsu had been active as a Japanese-style painter, entering competitions and exhibiting in group shows. In contrast, Orié had worked at a design firm for several years, and once she had learned the ropes, she went out on her own. These days, she was an independent illustrator, juggling commissions and selling her own pieces and merchandise.

But it wasn't enough to make a living. The income from her part-time jobs went into buying materials, and she struggled to break even. She imagined Mitsu had struggled plenty herself before winning this award.

That was why Orié was happy for her.

"It's a beautiful painting. I adore these colors," she said, examining the piece carefully.

Orié liked animation and cute illustrations, but her interest extended to all sorts of art, even beyond the genre she worked in. She had been a painting major, after all. Seeing the complex shades of green, she was inspired to incorporate those tones into her own work.

"What are you up to these days, Orié?"

Orié stiffened for a moment before answering.

"I take commissions for portraits online and at events. I also design merch, and this morning I've been helping out at my friend's stall at an event."

"I see. You've been working so hard all these years,

huh? Your characters are so cute—I've always loved them. I always knew they would become big hits."

"Big hits . . . I'd say I'm still pretty far from that." She tried to smile, but her cheeks twitched instead. "I also work part-time at several jobs."

"Me, too. I work night shifts doing quality inspection at a factory. There's no way you can survive on art alone."

But you won't have to from now on, will you?

Orié was stunned by the words that came into her head.

To live solely off your art, you had to become a fairly famous artist or work for a corporation. She had no idea how much prestige Mitsu would gain from winning this prize, but reality wasn't so kind as to allow living purely from your art to happen so quickly.

"Are you still in touch with your other art-school friends?" Mitsu asked. "I haven't been in touch with mine recently, and honestly, you're the only one I invited. I don't know why, but I felt a little awkward about getting in contact again."

Mitsu seemed a bit lonely. And she was still very shy.

There had been all sorts at art school—students who were outrageously eccentric, some who were terribly reserved, and those like Mitsu, who were serious and worked steadily. Orié had been an optimistic, dreamer type—always on the move, always surrounded by friends.

"I do keep in touch, or rather, I live with Umeka and Aimi."

"Really? That's nice. Sounds fun."

At the mention of her classmates' names, shy Mitsu looked envious. Orié guessed that she dedicated all her time to her part-time job and creating art, and would be doing so even now that she had won the prize. While Orié was also busy with work, she had fun in both her social and her work life. She felt some sympathy for Mitsu, who seemed to have a limited social life.

"Do you want to come over to our place sometime?"

"Can I?" Mitsu's face lit up. "Yes! I'd love to. I'd love to see Umeka and Aimi, too."

"Great. I'll be in touch. You're probably busier than I am, so it can be whenever you have time."

Although Orié had brought this up herself, she somehow couldn't bring herself to look Mitsu, who seemed so happy now, directly in the eyes. When she looked away, her gaze landed on Mitsu's painting.

Deep green mountains. Simple yet beautiful. She

could never paint anything like this. It wasn't a question of skill; comparing her art to this wouldn't make sense, because she and Mitsu worked in different genres. She understood that, but nonetheless, she felt a strange ache in her chest.

"You're looking pretty rough, Orié," said Umeka, one of her roommates.

Orié was aware of it. She nodded, her face clouded with gloom. "I know."

"If you know, then do something about it. You haven't eaten properly, like, in ten days, no? You've lost weight . . ."

"I'm on a diet."

"No, you're not. You've been like this since you went to Mitsu's exhibition."

Umeka had hit the nail on the head. Orié turned away. She had spent the entire day lying on the sofa in their living room, covering her head with a cushion, squeezing and wrestling with it—unable to sit still. Umeka probably just hadn't been able to watch in silence any longer.

"It wasn't much of an exhibition. It was held at a small gallery. A place that size, even I could . . ." As she spoke, she felt so pathetic that tears began to well up. Because she was lying down, the tears immediately spilled from the corners of her eyes.

"See, you're seriously in the dumps." Umeka found some space for herself on the end of the couch. "You've taken time off from your delivery job, right? How about your online orders?"

"I go to my café job. There's no one who can cover for me, so they've asked me to come in. As for my online shop, I posted a note saying I'm taking a little break. It's not like I get any orders anyway."

"Don't you have a solo booth at the flea market the month after next? You'll need a lot of work to sell, and you haven't started preparing for that at all."

"Don't tell me what I already know."

Orié pressed the cushion to her face to hide her tears, but she knew she wasn't really hiding anything.

Orié shared a three-bedroom apartment with her art-school friends, Umeka and Aimi. Back when she lived at home, she had felt her parents' disapproving glances whenever she had left to go to an event or a convention.

Since graduating from art school, all she had done was draw portraits that didn't make any money. To her parents, it seemed like she was just wasting her time.

Now, even though she had to share her living space, she had independence and room to breathe. Her two roommates had similar lives—supporting themselves with part-time gigs while pursuing their creative work.

Umeka taught glasswork and sold stained-glass trinkets. Aimi worked in traditional Japanese crafts. These days, she was creating objets d'art from driftwood and riverbed pebbles. Many of their former classmates had regular office jobs or were married with kids. They lived stable lives, but they had strayed from the dreams they had as students. Orié and her roommates were among the few who had pursued their art, their eyes focused on the path they had chosen. The same was true of Mitsu.

"It's a drag when you're down. Aimi won't say anything, but she's worried, too. She sent this without saying anything about it."

Orié looked up from behind the cushion and found Umeka's phone in front of her. She sniffled as she read the words on the screen. "'East of Takoyakushi Street, south of Tominokoji Street, west of Rokkaku Street, north of Fuyacho Street, Nakagyō Ward, Kyoto.' That's an odd address."

"It's not an exact location, but it's somewhere around there," said Umeka. "Aimi apparently heard about this mental health clinic from someone or other. Why not pay it a visit? When people in our line of work dig themselves into a hole, it can be hard to pull ourselves out of it, because we don't have something solid to stand on in the first place."

"That's not true. We have our dreams," said Orié.

"Dreams aren't ladders that help you climb out of a hole."

"You sound like a therapist, Umeka. Maybe you can listen to my problems?"

Orié straightened up on the couch. She and Umeka were the same age, but Umeka was levelheaded and acted as leader in their shared-living setup.

Umeka shook her head. "I'm not in a position to be happy about other people's successes either. I'm sure I'm thinking the same thing you are, so we'd just end up bad-mouthing others, putting ourselves down, then feeling miserable about it afterward."

"Umeka . . ."

"Aimi's the same way. So if the typically easygoing Orié stops being easygoing, it throws us off balance. Why not talk everything out with the doctor at the mental health clinic and come back feeling better?"

"It feels like half the stuff I said already was just slander."

"The truth is not slander," said Umeka, then disappeared into her room.

Orié let go of the cushion. If she wasn't careful, she was going to lose her sense of direction.

Everyone was in the same boat.

She had never been to a mental health clinic before, and despite having had to brace herself for this visit, it had been easy to walk into the examination room.

A man about her age was waiting inside. His kind face had no distinguishing features and would be tricky to capture in a drawing. The nurse from earlier would be easier to draw. She had cool eyes and a sharp nose. Orié had almost wanted to ask her to sit for her.

"Hello! It's your first time at our clinic, isn't it? How did you hear about us?"

The doctor's gentle questions snapped Orié out of

her thoughts. She had a bad habit of looking for distinctive features in people's faces.

"From a friend."

"I see. We're not accepting new patients at this time, but since you're a referral, we'll make an exception," said the doctor, smiling.

When he beamed, he seemed more approachable—almost charming. Although it was their first meeting, Orié felt at ease with him.

"Your name and age, please."

"Orié Onodera. I'm thirty."

"What brings you here today?"

She had thought about what to say before coming. She had no appetite, no energy, no motivation.

But she knew what was behind it all—her narrow-mindedness and jealousy.

So what was the remedy?

Find a stable job? Switch to an artistic discipline that had better prospects?

Or if she kept going with what she was doing, would there come a day when she would be rewarded for her work?

What did she want? Compliments? Or something more concrete, like winning a prize?

Before she could answer the doctor's questions, her own self-interrogation whirled in her mind. She couldn't even properly organize the problems she wanted to discuss. How she hated herself for this.

"I just don't know what to focus on anymore."

"I see," said the doctor. He began typing away on his keyboard. "We'll prescribe you a cat. The reason your vision is unfocused is that the people around you are a bit clouded, too. In situations like this, it's best to rely on a professional cat that works for anything right from the get-go. Tell me, Ms. Onodera, are you the type who would return something that someone had lost? Or are you the type to whisker it away for yourself?"

"Huh?"

"By the way, 'whiskering away' refers to when a cat, after finishing its business, becomes so hyped-up that it zooms around, wild with joy. Finding a lost item is exciting! Makes you want to whisker it away, doesn't it?"

The doctor was smiling again.

Orié froze. Why on earth was he asking that? She couldn't make sense of it at all. She hadn't whiskered anything away. She didn't really know what he was getting at, but she knew she hadn't done anything like that.

"I'm the type to return something . . ."

"Ah, so you're in that camp, eh? I see. In that case, let's go with a cat that's a pro among pros. Chitose, please bring the cat."

He called out to the curtains in the back of the room, and the nurse came through. In her hands was a plastic pet carrier.

"Dr. Nikké, normally we'd need to pay pro cats a special fee."

"Oh, is that so?" He giggled. "But in honor of Ms. Onodera, a type who doesn't whisker things away, just put it on my tab. I'll settle it eventually."

"No skipping out on the tab."

The nurse was prickly. She placed the carrier on the desk and walked off.

Orié felt herself tensing up. She'd come to a psychiatric clinic, and yet here she was feeling anxious. What was going on?

The doctor was still smiling, as if this disturbing conversation had not taken place, and swiveled the carrier around. The mesh panel now faced her, and she felt a gentle ripple in the air.

White, fluffy fur bobbed softly, as if stirred by a breeze. *A breeze?* Inside the carrier was a white, long-haired cat.

"A-adorable."

"*Right?*" said the doctor proudly. "You can see why she charges a special fee."

Orié still had no idea what he meant, but she was astonished by how cute the cat was. The fineness of her fur was impressive, and her features were also almost too perfectly formed. Her eyes, raised at the corners, were shaped like leaves. Her snout was pure white, and the edges of her ears were a burned brown. Orié had drawn a portrait of a cat of this breed before. A Ragdoll, if she remembered correctly.

"Take this cat for ten days. I'll write you a prescription, so please pick up what you need at reception. This cat can be highly codependent, so you might experience some interesting symptoms, but that's no cause for concern. Please give the people around you a heads-up as well. Any side effects are just proof that your body is working hard. Just get along with her as best you can. Well then, it's about time . . ."

"Huh?"

"Oh, yes! If you see a patient with an appointment waiting outside, please tell them to come in. The patient I'm expecting found something that had been lost but can't bring themselves to either return it or whisker it away. They're beating themselves up over it. You'll be fine, Ms. Onodera, as you're the type to return things. Now, take care."

The doctor's expression was kind, though something about it seemed distant. Time spent drawing so many faces had taught her to recognize it: he was the type who could smile or get angry without revealing the various emotions swirling within him. That was why she had no idea what he was thinking.

He'd be a challenging one to draw.

The doctor flashed Orié an affable smile and pressed the pet carrier into her hands. It was heavy and, most importantly, it contained a cat. She knew this wasn't something she should take on without serious consideration. And yet, unable to resist the strange pressure, she walked out of the examination room with it.

Just outside the door was an armchair, but there was no one sitting in it.

"Ms. Onodera?" a voice called. A pale hand beckoned from the reception window. It was the brusque nurse from earlier. Orié passed over the prescription and received a paper bag in return.

"These are your supplies," said the nurse. "There's an instruction leaflet inside—please read it carefully."

The bag contained kibble, a litter box, and other supplies for caring for a cat. Only then did Orié finally understand that she truly had been prescribed a cat.

"Um, I've, uh, never had a cat before, so I don't know how to take care of one."

"If there's anything you're not sure about, please ask the doctor. Take care," the nurse replied, then turned back to her paperwork, her face expressionless.

Earlier, Orié had thought this woman would be easier to draw, but now she thought the opposite might be true. She couldn't picture her smiling, and she seemed challenging to capture. What would her mouth look like? Would her eyes soften, or would they narrow?

The apartment she shared with her roommates was pet-friendly, but she knew that bringing a cat home suddenly like this would be a problem. She thought the leaflet might include thorough instructions on caring for a cat, but all she found was a single sheet of paper.

> **NAME:** Tangerine. Female. Four years old. Feed moderate amounts of food in the morning and at night. Water bowl must always be full. Clean kitty litter as needed. She can generally be left alone without is-

> sue. She is mild-mannered and easy to care for, but her emotions are hard to read, so vigilant observation is necessary. She must be brushed daily. Please use a brush appropriate for long-haired cats. That's all.

Orié tilted her head in confusion. The leaflet explained nothing. This wouldn't do.

"Excuse me, but do you have a more detailed instruction leaflet?" she asked the nurse.

"If there's anything you're not sure about, please ask the doctor." The nurse didn't even raise her eyes from her work.

Orié rummaged in the paper bag. She didn't know much about caring for animals, but it looked like everything she might need was there.

"Hmm?"

"Take care."

"The brush for long-haired cats . . ."

"Yes?" The nurse furrowed her brows.

"The leaflet says to use a brush appropriate for long-haired cats, but there isn't one in here. Should I buy one? Would one from the hundred-yen discount store be okay?"

The hundred-yen store was indispensable for sourcing

materials for artwork. If you needed items in bulk, you could go to a wholesaler, but if you only needed a few items, the hundred-yen store was the place to go. Quality aside, you could usually find just about everything there.

The crease between the nurse's eyes deepened. Though she was a beautiful woman, she looked terribly stern.

"Please wait a moment."

She disappeared from the reception window and returned after a moment holding a rectangular brush.

"This is the brush the cat uses every day. Please don't forget to bring this with you when you return the cat."

It was shaped like a small deck brush. Although it looked fairly new, there were already a few thin white fur strands entwined in its bristles. It seemed like someone had just brushed the cat.

How is this clinic set up? Do they also offer cat grooming here?

As Orié contemplated the brush, the nurse repeated in a sharp tone, "Take care."

Even through the mesh panels, the Ragdoll's fur seemed to shimmer, as if ruffled by a soft breeze.

When she got back to the apartment, Orié let Tangerine out into the room.

The cat filled the space with an almost divine presence. With her dense yet delicately tapered fur, her silhouette appeared almost hazy.

"This cat's got a halo around her," said Umeka, sounding half stunned.

Orié had thought the same thing.

Tangerine wasn't pure white. Between her eyes and up to her forehead she was cocoa colored, and so were the tips of her ears and her tail. Orié had always pictured cat tails as long and skinny, but Tangerine's was as bushy as a squirrel's.

When Orié settled down on the sofa, she told Umeka what had happened at the clinic. Umeka frowned as she listened, but she believed Orié's story.

"Who would have thought a psychiatrist would give you a cat to look after, and one that's almost Buddha-like?"

"I know. She's definitely glowing, right?"

They watched Tangerine from afar. She wandered around the living room for a while before calmly settling in front of the sofa. The only thing that moved was her fluffy tail, softly swaying back and forth.

This treatment has amazing visual effects.

"I was surprised, too. It was my first time at a mental

health clinic. You know, cats are supposed to be comforting—I bet this is a pretty common treatment method. They even gave me a full set of supplies to look after her."

"I don't know about *common*." Umeka tilted her head, though her gaze stayed fixed on Tangerine. "But it seems like you're back to your old carefree self."

"Look, she's going to her food bowl."

Orié had searched online for advice and had prepared the food, water, and litter box. Tangerine approached her bowl and slowly crunched one mouthful of the kibble, then another. But before long, she resumed her sitting position, her tail again the only thing that moved.

"Such a light eater . . ."

"Maybe she doesn't like the food?"

"Maybe it's the bowl the clinic gave me—that could be the problem. It looks kinda cheap."

"Aren't you supposed to be her servant? Maybe you should get her a ceramic plate or something."

"Servant? Who are you calling a servant? And ceramic—like fancy china that people use for tea parties? That stuff's expensive."

"They've got something like that at the hundred-yen store."

As they talked in hushed voices, as if not to disturb Tangerine's elegiac presence, Aimi, their other roommate, came through the door.

"Bad news," she announced. "The worst, actually. An exhibitor in my group show has come down with something and can't present their work anymore. If I don't find something substantial to fill the spot quickly, there's going to be a huge empty space."

She threw herself onto the sofa, sending the pillows bouncing.

Tangerine barely looked up.

"Wow, this needle-felted cat is insanely detailed. Who made it? And it moves. Is it battery powered? Wow, needle felting has come a long way."

Tangerine let out a short meow.

"It even makes sounds. Which one of you made this? If I can't create something in time for the upcoming show, maybe I'll take this piece. For now, I'm going to try and finish what I was working on for my next show and exhibit it at this one."

Tangerine stood up and padded over to her water bowl. Her steps were quiet, and it was as if she were floating. Aimi's eyes widened.

"Wait. Is it *real*?"

"Yup," answered Orié. Curious to see how Tangerine drank water, she lay flat on the floor. "Isn't she just like a stuffed toy? I got her from a clinic in Nakagyō Ward that Umeka told me about. She's so well-behaved. They say she's a pro."

"Is 'pro' her breed?" asked Aimi.

"No, she's a Ragdoll."

"I don't get it. That's an actual cat. I used to have a cat growing up, but it was . . . somehow different."

"You used to have a cat, Aimi?"

Orié was relieved. She felt reassured that one of them had some experience looking after a cat, but Aimi looked dubious.

"My family's cat was a stray that just showed up at our house and ended up staying, so it was never that friendly. This cat is a fluffball. Our cat was more like *hiss*, *grrr*, and *zoom*."

"That's just a bunch of sound effects," said Umeka, also watching Tangerine from the floor. "Do you think she'd mind if I petted her?"

"Of course she'll mind. She'll hiss at you."

"*Really?* Will she bite?

"I don't think she'll bite, but she'll hiss for sure."

"Why would she hiss?" asked Umeka. "Servant, may

I touch that little fluffy part of the cat's neck, just for a second?"

"Are you talking to me?" Orié recoiled slightly.

"Well, you're the one who brought her here. I think it'll be fine. The fur around her neck is so fluffy she won't even notice if I touch her there."

"Of course she'll notice. How could she not?"

The three of them kept whispering as they gradually closed in. Tangerine sat upright, her tail swaying back and forth her only movement.

Steeling herself to be bitten, Orié reached out her hand. There seemed to be no separation between Tangerine's head and body, and the area where her neck should have been looked like a white scarf wrapped around her neck multiple times. Orié wasn't sure where she was allowed to touch the cat, but her fingers felt like they were being pulled in toward the highest point around her neck.

Warm air brushed against her fingers.

Air? No, that's not it. There's the slightest hint of something. Cat fur? But there's nothing there.

"Oh no! My hand! It won't reach! I'm stuck!" she exclaimed.

"You're making zero sense."

"There's nothing there! Just fur!"

"Your vocabulary is pathetic."

Orié's fingers kept sinking in deeper and deeper. The fur around Tangerine's neck was thicker than it appeared. Orié no longer cared if she was about to be hissed at, and scooped up Tangerine with both hands.

"She's surprisingly heavy!"

Tangerine's fur was so long that Orié couldn't tell where to place her hands to support her properly. But as she drew Tangerine slowly into her arms, the cat neither hissed nor resisted. She went limp, her body dangling loosely. It felt like holding a sleeping child.

"Wow, this cat doesn't seem to mind being held at all."

Aimi gazed with nostalgia in her eyes, as if she were remembering her family's cat.

"Do you want to pet her—Aimi? Umeka?"

"Yes! I want to!"

"Me, too!"

They gathered around Tangerine, who was now sitting on Orié's lap, and gently stroked her.

Who knew cats could be this affectionate and adorable? When Aimi did some research, she found out that Ragdolls were famous for their gentle personalities and stunning looks, and how easy it was to look after them. Orié had drawn cats countless times on commission, always making them look extra cute, with the corners of their mouths lifted to make it seem like they were smiling. But no, she was the one smiling now. The corners of her mouth rose automatically.

It wasn't just Tangerine's cute appearance. There was a solid weight to her that a painting or photo couldn't capture. Underneath the seemingly endless sea of long fur, there was life. Feeling Tangerine's weight and warmth against her, Orié wondered if she could capture this in a drawing. The cat's aura. The softness of her fur, translucent in the light.

This was a problem that went beyond a creative slump. Capturing the feeling that brings a smile to a person's face—that wasn't something you could achieve through technical skill alone. Orié had no idea what it would take to achieve that.

The café where Orié worked part-time was old-school. You could call it a traditional coffee shop establishment, but it wasn't charmingly retro or stylishly vintage—it was just plain old. The handwritten menu had yellowed, and a random autograph was tacked up on the wall. Most of the customers were regulars. On the rare occasion a first-time visitor wandered in, they'd take one look around, decide it wasn't their thing, and walk straight out.

So business was slow. She was grateful she could work on her illustrations and merch when there were no customers around. The café manager was also kind enough to let her take walk-in portrait commissions. That said, only a small sign by the register advertised her services, and customers rarely asked for them. So far, she'd drawn portraits of the regulars' grandchildren, their children's wedding photos, and pictures of neighborhood kids.

The doorbell rang out lazily. Orié's hand, which had been sketching a miniature illustration, paused.

"Welcome."

A woman walked in. She wore a lilac kimono and had her hair pulled back. Her unadorned but neat attire made it clear at a glance that she was a geisha. When she scanned the café, Orié was sure she'd turn around, disappointed. But the woman's eyes paused on the small sign by the register.

"Excuse me, may I request one of these?" she asked.

"What? A portrait?"

"Yes." The woman gave a serene smile. "I saw on your website that you were taking a break from online orders, but since I was in the area, I thought I'd stop by. Are you still accepting commissions here?"

"I am, yes. Please come in."

Orié led the woman to a table by the window. It was highly unusual for someone to travel all the way to the café to commission a portrait. Her heart danced with excitement. The woman ordered a coffee. Orié set up her paper and colored pencils while her manager prepared the customer's drink.

The woman was bathed in the soft light filtering in through the window. The old table and wooden window frame had a character that perfectly complemented her kimono. The composition was so evocative Orié didn't want to draw a stylized caricature but a full, realist portrait.

In her mind, she pictured the finished work on a gallery wall. A gold plaque shone beneath it. If she was going to win a prize, it might as well be a prestigious one.

"Would you be able to draw from a photograph, as you did before for my little sister?"

The woman's query snapped Orié out of her thoughts.

Orié quickly arranged her face into a smile.

"Of course. Your sister, you said? What was her drawing like?"

"Here it is." The woman held out her phone. The screen displayed a portrait Orié had uploaded to her website. Three faces—Yuriha with her Shimada hairstyle; Shizue, the proprietress; and Mimita, the oval-faced cat.

"Oh, does your sister own Mimita?"

"Yes. Well, she's my honorary 'sister' in the sense we're both geiko at the same okiya. My name is Abino. The portrait of Mimita you drew for Yuriha was so lovely I wanted to ask for one, too."

"So that's why you came all this way . . . thank you so much."

She began to regret having stopped taking online requests.

The coffee was brought to the table. Abino added sugar and stirred it with her spoon so gracefully—every movement made for a perfect composition. Long, slender eyes and a sharp nose. Her beauty was not extravagant but refined.

"Oh? Abino . . ."

There was something familiar about her cool, composed face. *That nurse!* Abino looked so similar, in fact, that Orié could easily have mistaken one for the other.

Still, they couldn't be the same person. Because Orié knew she could draw Abino. If she lifted the corners of her reserved smile just a bit and added a light pink to her cheeks for a subtle glow, she'd have a warm and smiling portrait of this woman.

"Yes?" Abino peered into Orié's eyes.

"Oh, it's nothing," Orié replied quickly. "Do you have a picture of Mimita?"

"I have plenty," said Abino, showing Orié her phone. She'd saved dozens of images from every angle—from full-body shots to close-ups of his face.

"Mimita is so photogenic. His gaze is spot-on."

The ohagi-like Mimita worked the camera like a child model, giving it coy glances and perfect angles. Tangerine, back at the apartment, did exactly the same.

Mimita's eyes were ochre, while Tangerine's were a grayish blue. Even in photographs, their eyes were beautiful, like gems.

"Cats are so cute, aren't they? I'm taking care of one at home right now, and my roommates and I are always competing for her attention."

"Oh, really? I understand. We're constantly fighting over Mimita's attention at our place, too."

Abino giggled. Although her reserved manner made her appear older, she was likely only in her twenties. She was young, but there was a melancholy about her, and also an allure.

Orié felt compelled to capture Abino in a straightforward, traditional portrait. For a moment, she let her mind wander. *I went to art school and was classically trained in painting. If I'd gone down the orthodox path, maybe, by now, I'd be highly regarded, like Mitsu. I might be working on canvas rather than sheets of paper.*

But it was just a silly fantasy. Feeling a touch gloomy, Orié looked at Mimita's image on the phone screen. Abino had gone out of her way to come here. Orié needed to draw something that would satisfy her.

"Would you like a portrait of you and Mimita, with your faces side by side?"

"Mimita and—" Abino pulled up another image on her phone. "This one."

It was a calico, its white undercoat marked with patches of black and orange red. Its face was a mix of brown and black, highlighted by a striking white blaze running down its nose. Perhaps because of its slender build, it gave the impression of being haughty.

"What a beautiful cat. A calico?"

"Yes. Her name is Chitose. She's no longer with us, but could you include her in the portrait as well?"

"Of course."

By "no longer with us," did she mean that the cat had passed away?

Orié didn't ask. Instead, she had Abino swipe through a few photos on her phone. Every picture of Chitose the calico dated back to about two years ago.

But there was an issue—there were plenty of images, but in each one the cat was looking away. Even where her face was looking toward the camera, her eyes were clearly focused elsewhere.

"Do you not have one of her looking straight at the camera?"

"I don't," said Abino, sounding apologetic. "Whenever I took her picture, she was always like this—looking somewhere else. Normally, she'd stare right at you if you caught her eye, but when it came to photos . . . she really had such a contrary personality! Will it be a problem if you don't have a picture of her looking straight on?"

"No, that's fine. I'll pick out a few photos and draw her so it looks like she's facing this way. Which collar would you like her to wear? There are a few different colors."

She pointed to a red one. "This is the color that suited her best." Abino, who had been laughing so heartily, suddenly let her smile fade. It seemed she'd realized that she'd been speaking in the past tense.

"I wish I'd taken more pictures," she said as she gazed at the photo. "I can't get any more photos of her now. And I don't have a single one of her with Mimita. But in a portrait, the two could be shown together. If they had come together in real life, they might have ended up in a fight, but in an illustration, they can be friends."

As Abino stared at her phone, her sad expression softened and her eyes grew gentle. She was probably looking at a picture of the calico. A quiet giggle escaped her lips.

"Isn't she so cute?" she said into her phone.

Whom was she speaking to?

It was the first time Orié had seen eyes so clearly filled with love. This was how people looked when they experienced something that brought them joy.

Will I be able to draw them properly?

Flustered, Orié opened her case of colored pencils. This was her specialty, the field she had devoted herself to and believed in for so many years. If she couldn't pull herself together now, it felt like everything she'd built could come crashing down.

She produced the rough sketch with more brio than usual, Abino in the center, Mimita to her right. She gave the cat a round form and used a cheerful, cute color palette. To set it apart from the portrait she had done for Yuriha, she changed the angle a little. The result was a playful and charming portrait.

But as she began drawing Chitose the calico, her hand froze. Orié had no trouble capturing the colors and the shape of Chitose's face. The problem was her eyes. In every photo, the calico seemed to be looking elsewhere. And now, on the page, Chitose still wouldn't look back at her.

Perhaps curious why Orié's hand had stopped moving, Abino asked, "Is everything okay?"

"Um . . ."

What should I do now?

Should she just push herself to finish the portrait? Technically, the drawing was almost complete. The owner wanted their beloved cat to look cute—the Chitose on the paper was very adorable.

But there was no emotion. It was just a plain drawing of a cat.

She couldn't imagine Abino breaking into a smile as she had just now when she saw this work. She had to breathe life into Chitose if her illustration was to be worthy of Abino's affection.

That was not something she could possibly do at this moment.

Orié found herself saying something, fully prepared to be turned down.

"Please let me take this drawing home. I just can't get it right, and I want to take some time to rework it."

Abino blinked and stared at her with a blank expression.

"Is it because Chitose's photos aren't right? Because there isn't a good one of her?"

"No, not at all. I'm just not capturing her properly. Even if I continued to draw her like this, it won't make you smile as you do when you look at her photo . . . I can't put it into words, but I don't want it to end up just as a flat, lifeless image."

"I'm not entirely sure, but is this what you might call

professional dedication?" Abino asked, her expression serious. Her curiosity seemed to have been piqued.

It wasn't exactly, but Orié didn't know how else to explain it, so she nodded.

"Something like that. Since it's my fault the portrait hasn't been completed, I won't charge you a fee. I'll send it to you when it's done. I will of course cover the postage as well."

"That won't do. You're a professional, so you must be paid properly. I don't mind if you need some time. Please work on the portrait until you're satisfied. Mimita and I will be waiting together," said Abino.

Orié took down Abino's address, promised that she would definitely finish the portrait, and then walked Abino to the door of the café.

In all honesty, Orié wasn't confident that she would be able to complete the portrait properly. A customer had gone to the trouble of coming here, and the illustrator could not illustrate. As she watched the relaxed taiko knot of the Nagoya obi recede into the distance, a wave of self-pity washed over her.

My gaze is so unfocused.

With a heavy heart, at the end of her shift she took the unfinished portrait home to her apartment.

For the past six days, there had always been someone in the living room playing with Tangerine. Or not so much playing with her as gazing at her. The roommates each had their own schedule. Some days they didn't emerge from their rooms at all, and on others, day and night were completely flipped.

Tonight, it was Umeka who was on the floor observing Tangerine as she sprawled out on the sofa. If there hadn't been a cat there, she would simply be a person lying on her back on the floor.

"Umeka, you scared me. I thought you'd fainted."

"Take a look at her from this angle," Umeka replied, gesturing for Orié to join her.

Orié rolled onto the floor and peered up at the sofa, gazing at Tangerine's face.

"Wow. Her cheeks are dango dumplings."

"Isn't her mouth also amazing? It's exactly like a caret."

"Like an up arrow. How can a face have both confectionery and punctuation on it?"

Orié stared mesmerized at the underside of Tangerine's chin. She was an exceptionally calm cat. Her movements were gentle, and she never caused any fuss, whether with her food, water, or litter box. Sometimes she'd approach with padded steps, but most of the time she lay on her side and didn't move much. With her ash-tinted blue eyes, she'd gaze serenely into empty space.

"What's caught your eye?" Orié muttered softly.

Tangerine's blue eyes often stared into space—into air, the wall, out through the window. It was unclear what drew her interest, but her focus never faltered. *Completely unlike mine*, thought Orié.

"Tangerine, shall I brush you?" said Umeka, moving onto the sofa. She traced Tangerine's back with the brush given to them by the clinic. Once she had worked through all the fur on Tangerine's back, she lifted the cat's front paws over her head as if in a victorious cheer.

"Orié, now her tummy."

"Yes."

Orié took hold of the brush. Even with her creamy stomach exposed, Tangerine showed no agitation. Her fur was thicker around her neck, but it was fluffy and looked light. The fur on her abdomen and around her legs was all tangled. They had brushed her only yesterday, but already the areas that rubbed together were matted, like a high-pile rug. The instruction leaflet had said that daily brushing was necessary, and it really was.

As they were vigorously brushing the cat, Aimi

emerged from her room. Her hair was even more disheveled than the fur around Tangerine's belly.

"Hey, that's not fair! You need to tell me when you're grooming her," said Aimi.

"But you're busy working on that additional piece."

"It's almost finished. Let me brush her, too."

Aimi knelt beside them. While Aimi brushed Tangerine, Orié stroked her fluffy tail. It felt so wonderful Orié thought she might just melt.

"Oh, right, I know this is sudden, but are either of you at home around this time tomorrow?" asked Aimi, still brushing the cat.

"Yeah, I'll be here," said Orié.

"Me, too. What's up?"

"Do you guys remember Mitsu? Mitsu Asakura? I heard that she won the Higashiyama something prize, so I got in contact with her. She said she wanted to come over. I thought maybe we could host a little party at our apartment—we haven't had one of those in a while—and celebrate her win."

She took a look at the brush and frowned.

"Cats shed so much fur. If this were my hair, I'd be crying."

Complaining to Aimi about Mitsu would be unreasonable. Orié hadn't even mentioned meeting Mitsu to Aimi, and saying she didn't want her to come over would just be selfish. After all, she was the one who had invited Mitsu in the first place.

Orié's eyes met Umeka's, and she gave an awkward smile, which Umeka returned. She smoothed things over as best she could and took Tangerine back to her room. They had agreed that Tangerine would sleep in Orié's room, since the others' rooms were filled with fragile things. For Tangerine's bed, Orié had lined an empty storage bin with sheets and blankets.

Tangerine hopped onto Orié's bed instead. Because she was big, the sofa and the bed seemed like the highest places she could leap onto, and she didn't seem inclined to climb onto anything taller.

Orié took her art supplies out of her bag. She carried them wherever she went. The illustration Abino had commissioned from her was also in her bag. It was nearly finished—the calico's markings and the placement of her eyes and nose, and the corners of her mouth, which were slightly upturned, as always, were all there. All that was left to do was to color in the eyes and capture the light bouncing off them so they would appear full of life.

The cat looked adorable, but that wasn't enough. No matter how hard she tried, she didn't feel like she could create a good portrait. There was a real cat in her room, yet she couldn't even use it as a reference. Orié felt at a loss.

Tangerine sat primly on the bed, her chin slightly raised as she stared at a spot on the wall. Her eyes rippled like the water's surface. But her gaze remained focused. She was staring at a blank wall, not a mark or speck of dust anywhere.

How is she able to stare so intently at nothing?

Orié felt her chest tighten. She didn't know what to focus on anymore. She didn't even know what it was that she wanted to see.

She nestled close to Tangerine and looked in the same direction. Of course, there was nothing there.

"What are you focusing on?" murmured Orié as she stared at the wall.

Tears blurred her vision. She had no idea where to direct her gaze. She could no longer see anything.

In the end, she couldn't bring herself to pick up her colored pencils that night.

The following day, Orié finished her café shift an hour early. Umeka and Aimi went shopping, while Orié was tasked with decorating the apartment. She had felt depressed last night, but now that she was in charge of the decor, her creative energy ignited. On top of that, there was a vast supply of materials she could use. In no time, she had transformed the walls and ceiling, and the apartment looked as festive as any party venue.

I would be thrilled if I won a prize and my friends celebrated with me. I'd feel that I was finally being rewarded for all my hard work.

Orié was pleased with the decorations she'd put up. Regardless of the emotions that lay beneath the surface, she was a professional after all, despite her flaws. She had, in the end, been able to put her skills to use.

There was another professional who also deserved praise.

"Tangerine, you're amazing."

While Orié had worked on the decorations, Tangerine had remained on her best behavior. With all the fluffy, fluttering decorations, even Tangerine had seemed like she was itching to play. Every so often, she had stood up, ready to pounce, but she hadn't got up to any mischief.

"You're such a good girl. Like that weird doctor said, you're a pro among pros."

Orié picked up Tangerine and nuzzled her face into the cat's neck. She could sink into it forever. Tangerine had been with them for eight days already. *I don't want to give her back*, Orié thought, taking a deep breath.

Umeka and Aimi returned, laden with bags of food. The three of them weren't great cooks, so they mainly bought prepared foods, some alcohol, and a cake. When they had first started living together, they had held lively gatherings all the time. Lately, though, they had been far too busy even to share a meal. This was their first get-together in a long time.

The instant Mitsu stepped into the apartment, her eyes gleamed.

"Wow, I am so happy. So, so happy."

Tears filled her eyes, and her shoulders trembled. Seeing her friend cry, Orié felt like crying, too.

As she had been spending all her time working at flea markets and making art, somewhere along the way she had forgotten the joy of sharing her life with her friends. When the four of them raised their glasses for a toast, she felt transported back to their art-school days. Back then, they had had no clear sense of direction or goals—they had just focused on doing what they loved and pursuing their passions.

"Oh my gosh! A *cat*!" exclaimed Mitsu, spotting Tangerine.

Tangerine padded over with elegant steps as if to say, *I was wondering when you'd notice me*. They had brushed her thoroughly for the occasion, so her coat had a lustrous shine.

"What a *beautiful* cat. I'm so jealous. I want a cat, but I'm worried it might break things or scratch me."

"Tangerine is so gentle. She's such a good girl."

"Really? I'd love to have a cat like her."

The four of them gathered around Tangerine, who lay stretched out on the sofa. They ate and drank, growing increasingly animated as they exchanged stories about the past, the present, and what the future held. All four were now pleasantly tipsy. Once the alcohol had kicked in, Mitsu became talkative and let out a few gripes. Winning the prize hadn't led to more job opportunities, and her circumstances remained unchanged.

"I figured this would happen, but a little part of me was hopeful. But I got zero press coverage or inquiries."

"So, you didn't start receiving loads of commissions the very next day, huh?" said Umeka with a sigh.

Mitsu, too, let out a sigh.

"Maybe someday, if we keep up the hard work. But even if we don't, in the end, we're doing this because we love it. I can't quit, even though I'm getting old. Even if nothing ever comes of it."

"True."

Umeka glanced at Orié, who responded with a faint smile.

They were all struggling with the mismatch between their age and where they were in life. They hadn't changed what they were doing, yet time was marching on. Orié knew exactly how Mitsu felt when she said she couldn't quit.

Just as things were starting to turn serious, there was a loud crash, as if something had shattered. They froze.

"What was that?" asked Umeka, her voice laced with fear.

That was undoubtedly not a good sound. Nervously, they looked toward the bedrooms and saw that the door to Aimi's room was slightly ajar.

"Really?"

Aimi ran to her room. She shoved open the door and gasped.

Standing behind Aimi, Orié peeked into the room. It was littered with wood panels, driftwood, and ceramics, as always. But the picture frame on the floor was clearly broken.

Tangerine had flattened herself on the very top of the shelf, in a sliver barely the width of a hand turned on its side. Her bushy tail dangled lazily toward the floor.

"It's ruined," said Aimi, letting out a loud sigh as she turned to look at the frame. It was a modern art poster. Pieces of cut glass and traditional Japanese blown glass had been affixed around the frame, and now those had shattered and embedded themselves into the poster. "I put it on top of the shelf to dry. Oh god. There's no hope for it now."

Aimi's shoulders slumped in despair. The sculpture, built around a picture frame as its base, was adorned with lace ribbons and feathers like the train of a dress. Although not entirely broken, several ornaments were damaged.

Careful not to step on the glass, Orié stretched two hands up to the shelf and slowly brought Tangerine down. The cat looked crestfallen, somehow.

"I'm sorry. It's my fault. I wasn't keeping an eye on her."

"It's not your fault, Orié," said Aimi through a strained smile. "It was my fault for not closing my door properly. I left fragile stuff lying out, even though we have a cat around. I'm sorry, Tangerine. It must have startled you."

Neither Aimi nor Tangerine was at fault—it was my mistake. Orié bit her lip, feeling guilty. Because Tangerine was so well-behaved, she hadn't been focusing on her properly—really paying attention. She probably wanted to pounce on frilly things and climb to high places, like any cat. Tangerine had been suppressing those urges. Orié buried her face in Tangerine's neck, her eyes brimming with tears.

"I'm so sorry, Tangerine."

"For now, let's put Tangerine in your room," said Umeka. "Aimi, isn't this the additional piece you were going to show at the exhibition tomorrow?"

"Yeah, but it is what it is. I'll stand in the empty spot myself, like a model. How's that for art, huh?" Aimi forced a laugh.

Orié, Umeka, and Mitsu exchanged looks.

"Aimi, we have four artists here," said Umeka. "Our

specialties may be different, but we've all been formally trained. I think we can come up with something a bit better than you standing there like a model. Right, Orié? Mitsu?"

"Yes!"

Aimi stared blankly for a second, then her eyes lit up.

"You're right. I'm starting to feel fired up. I'm feeling an urge to make something *amazing.*"

"Well, we don't have a ton of time, so it's going to be something average," said Umeka, shaking her head.

From that moment, they worked like a tornado. With great focus, they cut and pasted, drew and painted. Paint splattered their faces and clothes. Putting on gloves, they carefully restored the glasswork. They held their breath as they meticulously attached the feathers with tweezers.

It's how it used to feel. I'm still doing what I love.

We've all been focused. We've kept our eyes on what we love.

The result of such a collaboration of individual strengths was completed the next morning. Without having had a wink of sleep, Aimi left with the difficult-to-describe art object, while the other two crashed in the living room. Orié went back to her room. Tangerine, who was curled up in the storage bin, lifted her head and looked at her.

Her light blue eyes focused on one spot.

Ah, those eyes. So clear and unwavering.

As the drowsiness pulled her under, Orié felt she'd finally grasped something.

The last time Orié had come to this area, she had circled it several times. Just as she had been about to give up, she had spotted the alley. But today, curiously, she had found it very easily. When she pushed open the old metal door, she saw the reception window. The nurse was sitting behind it.

"Ms. Onodera, I see you're here to return the cat. The doctor is waiting for you. Please come in."

The nurse's tone was icy, and she didn't give Orié so much as a glance. She looked identical to Abino, who had commissioned the portrait, but her demeanor was utterly different.

Orié entered the examination room and found the doctor waiting for her.

"Aah, your complexion is healthy, and your aura seems good, too. Looks like that cat worked."

"Yes." Orié nodded. Tangerine was inside the carrier, which was now on the desk. White fur peeked out from the mesh panels on the side.

Thanks to Tangerine, her bond with Umeka and Aimi, and even Mitsu, had deepened. They may have been struggling in their own ways, but sharing in one another's triumphs and setbacks had allowed them to move forward together.

"I came to terms with the fact that it's okay if my gaze is unfocused. Even if what I was looking at yesterday is different from what I'm looking at today, as long as I'm doing what I love, that's fine. It's also acceptable to stare at nothing, like a cat."

"Oh my, she's talking about *you*," the doctor said with a mischievous, childlike grin as he lifted Tangerine out of the carrier.

The cat sprawled out on the desk and swayed her fluffy tail like a dusting brush.

"Cats, they tend to fix their gazes on what they love. That's what they're always focused on."

Orié blinked. Tangerine often stared at the wall and into empty air. Even when she was facing the window, her gaze was not on the scenery outside but on the windowpane.

"But she often just stares at nothing."

"To humans, it may seem like they're looking at nothing of any significance, but for cats, they are looking at something they love."

The doctor beamed.

Orié stared blankly at Tangerine. Her light blue eyes were translucent like marbles, and the object of her gaze was truly impossible to discern.

Suddenly, Tangerine turned to look at her.

Their eyes met.

Cats look at the things they love.

Orié gasped. "My phone."

"Yes?"

"The photos. The ones she sent me. I was convinced that—"

Orié retrieved her phone from her bag. The calico wasn't looking at the camera in any of the reference photos sent to her by Abino. Her gaze was directed a little above or away from the center, never straight ahead. Orié had assumed the cat was looking away because she didn't like the phone being pointed at her.

But that wasn't it.

"She's looking at her owner in every one of them."

Love, love, so much love.

Those eyes were focused on someone she loved. That was why they were turned away from the camera.

Orié hurriedly took out her art supplies from her bag. She had on her the shikishi art boards she used for sketching at the café.

"Would it be all right if I drew something here, right now? If I don't capture it immediately, it'll slip away."

The doctor laughed. "How very catlike of you. Sure, go ahead."

He placed Tangerine on his lap and stroked her with long, smooth movements.

"*So* silky. *So* nice. *So* wish you'd give us a discount on your fees."

As the doctor spoke to Tangerine, Orié began shading her portrait of the calico cat with colored pencils. *Eyes turned toward her. Eyes looking at what she loved.*

She could picture a laughing Abino holding her phone up to the calico and following her around to snap a cute photo. She had probably been smiling, her loving eyes fixed on the phone screen.

And the cat had been watching her.

". . . I'm done."

An unbidden breath escaped Orié.

She sighed under the gaze of the cat she had sketched.

Chitose, Abino, and Mimita were all looking her way and smiling.

"They are all so cute," she said.

"Truly. *So* cute. *So* kind. *So* wish you'd consider giving us a discount," said the doctor. "Oh, are you done? Yes? That's wonderful."

Without fanfare, the doctor placed Tangerine back in the carrier and called out toward the curtains at the back. "Chitose, please take the cat."

"Yes," said the nurse as she came into the room.

Orié, who had been lost in thought, snapped back to attention. Looking unconcerned, the nurse picked up the carrier.

Her aloofness seemed even more apparent, possibly because Orié couldn't help comparing her to Abino from the portrait. She found herself staring before she realized it.

"What is it?" asked the nurse, her brows knitted.

"Oh, um . . ." Orié was flustered. "I thought you looked just a bit like this person in the portrait."

They really did have similar features. When she turned the portrait toward the nurse, her eyes widened in surprise.

"Oh!"

Unexpectedly intrigued, she set the carrier back on the desk and leaned in toward the portrait.

"Do I look like that? Stars in my eyes and everything. How embarrassing!"

The nurse let out a charming laugh that was part bashful, part pleased. But then her expression suddenly turned serious and she looked down at the doctor with a cool gaze.

"Isn't the patient with an appointment going to be here soon? If you keep fooling around like this, your important patient might just leave. Don't blame me if that happens."

She took hold of the carrier and slipped behind the curtains.

Tangerine had disappeared all too quickly, leaving no trace or impression behind. It was as if it had all been a dream.

But Orié had lots of photos of Tangerine on her phone, and she could still feel the softness of her fur beneath her fingers. It most definitely had not been a dream.

She paused, then said, "Excuse me, Doctor?"

"Yes? What's the matter? Are you offering to split Tangerine's fee?"

"What? No. I would like to draw a portrait of Tangerine and post it on my website. Would that be okay?"

The doctor took a moment to reflect. "I think that would be fine," he said. "If they ask me about portrait rights or whatever, I'll just laugh it off. And if you ever find yourself not knowing where to focus your gaze, just look toward what brings you joy, just as cats do. Now, take care."

The doctor really did have a face that was difficult to capture. Orié walked out of the examination room. At the reception window, she dropped off the brush she'd borrowed, offering a new one as well.

"My friends and I chipped in to buy this. The bristle feel and size are the same, but if you press the button in the back, all the fur comes off at once. Since Tangerine sheds a ton, I thought she must be challenging to groom. Please use this, if you'd like to."

"Oh. Thank you very much," said the nurse, her voice flat. She took the brush.

That was it. Not even a hint of appreciation.

But she'd probably brush Tangerine beautifully. Both the doctor and the nurse were odd people, but Orié could sense that their kindness was sincere.

She turned the handle of the metal door and stepped

into the hallway. It was an old building with no elevator—quite a rarity these days. A man in a flashy shirt was on his way up the stairs.

Just as she was thinking, *He looks kind of dodgy*, he bounded up to her.

"Hey, you. Were you taking cat lessons, too?"

Orié froze, the question taking her by surprise. His face was also tense, as if he was seeing something that scared him, though, really, it was she who should have been afraid.

"No, I was not," she replied.

"*Really?* You weren't taking cat lessons?"

The man began to close in on her. Orié shrank back.

"No, I was not," Orié repeated. "I may not look like one at first glance, but I am an artist, and I can draw a cat without lessons."

". . . Draw a cat?" The man stood there, dumbfounded. His face was a flurry of changing expressions. "What does it mean when you say you can draw a cat?"

Is drawing a cat really such a strange thing? He couldn't seem to understand the point of a pet illustration. She sometimes came across people like him. Realizing he was no threat at all, Orié gave him her business card.

“I’m an artist, you see. I specialize in illustrations and portraits. Besides cats, I also draw people and other animals. If you’re interested in one, please check out my website.”

The man took hold of her card.

“Draw a cat . . .” he muttered in a daze.

Orié felt a touch of annoyance. *He doesn’t have to act so surprised.*

Illustration was a special thing, she was sure of it. Even just now, Nurse Chitose had finally broken into a smile, simply after seeing a portrait that looked just like her. To be able to draw out a smile like that—that was the charm of portraiture. Now that she came to think of it, Abino’s cat was also named Chitose, like the nurse. Both seemed standoffish.

Orié left the building, sidestepping the man, who stood frozen in place. The sky above was clear. Eager to deliver the portrait as soon as possible, she contacted Abino, who told her she could come right away. She walked twenty minutes from the Rokkaku-Tominokoji area to the entertainment district in Higashiyama. The stone-paved paths of Gion, lined with teahouses and traditional restaurants, exuded an old-world charm. At the last okiya in a row, Abino came out to greet her.

"Thank you for coming all the way," she said, smiling. A light brown tabby cat peeked out from between her feet. His ears were plastered to his oval-shaped head, and his legs were very short. "Here, Mimita, say hello to our guest."

Abino held up Mimita's short forepaws in the air as if he were cheering. The bell on his collar jingled. Orié had already seen photos of him when she had drawn Yuriha and Abino, but his real-life cuteness was in a class of its own.

"I've completed the portrait of Mimita and Chitose," said Orié, handing it over to Abino.

In the middle was Abino, with the two cats beside her. She'd also included their names. Compared to the real-life Mimita sitting before her, the portrait felt a little lacking, but nevertheless, she beamed with pride.

Abino stared intently at the portrait. Then a wide smile spread across her face.

"Oh my!" She giggled. "Chitose, so that's how you've been looking at me? Your eyes are sparkling." She hugged the portrait to her chest. "I'm so glad you're with Mimita. I'm glad you guys are getting along in this picture."

Orié didn't know what had happened to Abino's calico, but the eyes looking at Abino from the portrait were focused on something she loved. Whether cat or human, the gaze directed toward what you loved was the same.

"I'm so glad," she murmured again.

It was not Abino who began to weep but Orié. She felt a deep, earnest desire to keep drawing pictures that could bring such joy.

For now, she would capture the softness of Tangerine, whom she held firmly in her heart. She wanted to depict her so vividly that she appeared alive—so that anyone who viewed the portrait couldn't help but talk to the likeness, just as Abino had done with hers.

And once she'd finished the portrait, she'd go to the Nakagyō Kokoro Clinic for the Soul and show it to that weird doctor and nurse.

For the past few days, Akira Shiina had been feeling troubled.

The mysterious woman who had emerged from the neighboring unit had given him a business card. It had made him suspicious. At first glance, it looked like a typical card with her name and contact information.

Should I look her up? What should I do?

But perhaps it would be better not to get involved any

further. Something about the unit next door was definitely off. A shiver had gone down his spine when the cleaning woman had told him that she had found black cat fur in his office. To him, that was basically a sign of something paranormal.

"But . . . why should I be freaking out over something like this? It's got nothing to do with me. The cats next door were abandoned way before I moved in. That's right—no need for me to be scared. I have this mighty magnetic necklace. I can exorcise a business card or two with the power of magnets."

Shiina gripped the necklace that hung from his neck. Even among the necklaces he sold, this one was a top-tier piece. He'd debated getting the highest-grade model but had decided against it after taking the price into consideration.

Clutching his necklace, he typed in the URL on the business card. As the woman had said, it led to the website of an illustrator who showcased her work and artistic style.

At first glance, there was nothing particularly suspicious about it. But then he checked the blog and frowned. It featured a colorful illustration of humans and their cats. The women in it wore kimonos, and from their hairstyles it was clear that they were geiko. In fact, he recognized the woman in the portrait flanked by two cats. Her name was captioned below.

"Abino . . . wasn't that the woman who used to cry outside the unit next door?"

The illustration was manga-style, so it was hard to be certain it was her, but he became curious. He only vaguely remembered her, but she had been attractive and just his type. That was neither here nor there, but he couldn't shake the feeling that the woman wasn't unrelated to the woman in the picture.

The portraits were likely to be of the geiko from Hanamachi, the entertainment district. The first person who came to mind when he thought of that area was Ioka, the owner of this building. He'd heard that Ioka enjoyed living it up in Gion.

Should I try to talk to him?

Or should I avoid getting more involved?

Shiina tightened his grip around his necklace.

Cat shadows kept flickering in his mind. Magnetic power was undeniably effective for stiff shoulders, high blood pressure, and loss of appetite—but whether it worked on cats or not had yet to be tested.

For a start, what would count as "working" on cats?

Did cats even get stiff shoulders? Could magnetic powers reverse their aging? Would their whiskers multiply? Or maybe they'd grow a tail?

"No, that can't be right—they already have tails."

The more he tried to conjure in his mind what a cat tail really looked like, the stranger his thoughts became. *They curl up, maybe? Kinked at the tip?*

He sighed. It wasn't just cats that bored him—he had no interest in animals at all. It was all starting to become tiresome.

"How stupid. What do I know?"

Shiina grimaced and powered down his computer.

Shiro

4

Shiro

A mixture of frustration and nervousness made her want to back out even before she'd left her apartment. She headed west on Rokkaku Street, then turned down a random side street, guessing she was in roughly the right place. They had given her directions over the phone, but having rarely been to the narrow streets of Nakagyō Ward, she couldn't tell one from the other.

They all looked pretty similar, being made up of old town houses and narrow structures. When she spotted the five-story multipurpose building, the tension eased from between her brows.

It was closer to Shinkyōgoku and Shijō Streets than she'd thought, but in a shabby building like this, she was unlikely to run into anyone she knew. Inside, the hallway was lined with metal doors, the paint peeling. There was no elevator.

She climbed up the stairs to the fifth floor and knocked on the second door from the end. It was faint, but she could hear the sound of cats meowing. The door opened and, immediately, the cries intensified. A woman who looked younger than her mother appeared.

"Ms. Ao Torii?"

"Yes," she answered curtly.

The door swung open farther, revealing the room inside. It was bright and clean as a whistle. There was a distinct scent of animals, but it was nothing too bothersome. More than anything, it was the smell of milk that dominated.

"Were you able to find us easily? The streets around here are so confusing, aren't they?"

"Well, yes."

In fact, Ao had at first gone down the wrong street and ended up at an old private clinic located directly behind this building.

Ao spotted another woman standing on the other side of the room. She was wearing a faded sweatshirt, her hair was pulled back into a messy ponytail that hinted at a life of hard work, and she looked like she was in her mid-forties. The troubled look on her face made it clear she wasn't glad to see Ao.

"Isn't this girl a little too young, Ms. Asou?" the woman with the ponytail asked.

"Maybe," said Ms. Asou with a grimace.

It was with Ms. Asou that Ao had corresponded.

Ao silently surveyed the room. Wall-mounted racks were lined with cages, not the glass enclosures you might see in a pet store but ones with metal bars. There were four cats in cages and three more in the large playpen on the floor. The cats in the playpen tumbled about, chewing on blankets. Their small bodies and faces made them look very young. The place was full of kittens.

Before Ao could make herself look away, the woman with the ponytail stepped in front of her. "Thanks for coming, but you're still at school, right? This place . . . well, it's probably not the kind of job you're imagining. I don't think it's something a kid your age could handle."

"I'm not at school," Ao replied firmly.

The woman looked surprised.

Ao looked young because she dressed like a boy and kept her hair short. People often said her perpetually sullen expression made her seem like a moody child. And now the woman's unwelcome remark had put her in a bad mood, so her glare was sharper than ever.

"I didn't finish high school. I'm eighteen, though. Is that a problem? I was told the work involves picking up cat poop and pee, handling vomit, and cleaning all day. The cats might bite or scratch, and they might even die. Is that a good summary? Anything else I need to know?"

Ms. Asou's email had spelled out the hourly wage and working conditions, and she had even called Ao to let her know she had been hired. And yet, was this woman now trying to pretend none of this had happened, as adults liked to do on a whim?

If she wants to be angry, fine. Ao glared at her, her own ire showing.

But the woman with the ponytail laughed and said, "My goodness, you really talked up the job, huh, Ms. Asou? If you describe the job so plainly like that, no part-timer's going to want to work with us."

"That's why, even though we had lots of applications, she was the only one who didn't turn down the job," replied Ms. Asou. "Anyway, it would be a hassle if we hired someone who just complained and quit right away. That's why I made things sound a little worse than they actually are."

"In any event, cleaning all day isn't too far from the truth." The woman with the ponytail gave an exasperated laugh. "And yet, after hearing the job description, you still came? Are you a cat person?"

"Not particularly, but I like animals," said Ao.

"That's a given. You wouldn't apply for this job if you didn't like animals," Ms. Asou said with a smile.

Ao didn't return it.

She didn't actually like animals. But she did dislike people.

What she wanted was a job with decent pay that required minimal human interaction and couldn't be done from home. These days, job ads weren't allowed to specify gender or age, but positions such as warehouse staff and security guards were still tough for young women to land. She didn't have a driver's license, so delivery jobs were also off the table. If you weren't picky, there were plenty of part-time jobs to choose from, but finding one that met your specific skills could be challenging. Ao didn't mind where she worked so long as her conditions were met.

The woman with the ponytail examined Ao's inscrutable face intently.

"We specialize in cats, but unlike the pet shops in town, we raise our cats here in this building, so it's pretty closed off. Since the shop is more of a hobby for the owner, the cats tend to stay here for a while before finding homes. It means you end up growing quite attached to them, and it's hard when it's time to say goodbye. If you truly love animals, you should consider this carefully . . ."

"That's enough, Ms. Hase," said Ms. Asou with a frown. "This girl is adamant that she wants to work here. Ms. Torii, the work is exactly how I described in the email. We have two people working each shift, so that means working weekends and holidays—is that okay with you?"

"Yes," Ao answered simply.

Ms. Asou nodded.

"Until the owner of the business comes back, I've been put in charge, but in reality, Ms. Hase outranks me. Isn't that right?" She looked over at the woman with the ponytail.

"I do not," said Ms. Hase with a weak smile. "I just work part-time."

The two women were similar in age but had very different demeanors. Ms. Asou appeared polished, with long nails and blow-dried hair that weren't suited to animal care. In contrast, Ms. Hase was dressed more practically.

While Ao was reviewing and filling out various documents, the cats in the playpen started to fight and were now meowing threateningly at one another. The three kittens became a tangled ball of fur, tumbling over one another.

"Hey! Mugi, Choco—stop it!"

Ms. Hase pulled out the two brown kittens by the scruffs of their necks As if a switch had been flipped, they instantly stilled. Ms. Hase's handling had been swift and firm. The kittens, now swinging aloft, let their front paws dangle loosely, and their expressions relaxed. It was as if they had become soft toys.

Ao was aware that mother cats often held kittens by their scruffs, but it was the first time she'd actually seen it done. The way the skin stretched around the kitten's neck looked uncomfortable.

"Doesn't it hurt them when you hold them like that?" Ao asked, frowning.

Ms. Hase laughed and swung her ponytail. "Not if

you do it right. Don't do it for too long or when they become heavier," she said. "Kokubei, you're always getting picked on. You're the older brother, you know?"

She addressed the kitten now in the corner of the pen. He was black from the tip of his ears to his tail. Only his eyes were gray.

"These kittens are around four months old. The ones over there are a bit younger."

Ms. Hase placed the two kittens in a cage and indicated with a glance the cardboard boxes at the back of the room.

When Ao craned her neck, she could see two slightly smaller kittens asleep inside—a calico and a tabby.

"Aren't they cute?" asked Ms. Hase.

Ao nodded.

Ms. Hase moved the black kitten from the pen over to a cage and began to dismantle the playpen. The sheet that had been laid beneath it was covered in poop and pee. It seemed that "cleaning all day" hadn't been an exaggeration.

Ms. Asou had finished reviewing the employment documents.

"All right. Now you can start working for us. Ms. Hase, please show Ms. Torii the ropes. I need to pick up my kid from cram school," she said, before quickly disappearing through the door.

Ms. Hase seemed unconcerned to be suddenly left with a new hire who knew nothing.

"Ms. Asou handles the finances and our storage space. I'm Misato Hase. I work part-time, and you're likely going to be paired up with me on most shifts. Nice to meet you."

"Sure. Now, tell me what I need to do," said Ao matter-of-factly. Regardless of the circumstances, she had no interest in engaging with people any more than necessary. Most people bristled at her attitude, and she was used to that. Misato, however, remained smiling.

"You're motivated—that's good. The owner will be back next month, and we can go over your shifts then. I'm sure there are days you will want to go out with your friends."

"Probably not."

"Oh, okay. Well then, I'm sorry to put you to work right away, but can you help me prepare their food? Kittens need to be fed frequently, so it's a lot of work."

Ao followed Misato's instructions and prepared the cats' food. It wasn't as simple as just scooping it into bowls. Their diets varied depending on their age, even on their build. Some needed special toppings or ingredients mixed in.

After preparing a bowl for each cat, Ao opened the cage door to slip the dish inside. One cat tried to slither out through the gap, and Ao quickly pushed it back in.

How did that happen? By the laws of physics, the gap was far too narrow for the cat to fit through, yet somehow it had nearly squeezed its way out. From then on, she took the cat's size into account before opening the cage door. Again, through a three-centimeter gap, a five-centimeter cat head would peek out.

Are cats . . . molluscs?

Ao stood there, perplexed.

"Ms. Torii, have you ever owned a cat?" Misato asked, amusement in her voice.

"N-no, I haven't."

The cats followed Ao's hands, darting back and forth as if doing a lantern festival dance. Their movements were adorable, but Ao's goal was simply to feed them. She distracted them with one hand while sliding the bowls into the cages with the other. Every time she tried to put a bowl in, a cat would make a dash for the opening. When she tried to push the cat gently back inside, it would hook its claws into her sleeve and hang on tightly. After several incidents like this, her sleeve became stretched and worn.

After a lot of effort, she finally got all the bowls of food into the cages. The cats moved in unpredictable ways. Some flipped over their bowls the moment they were placed inside. Misato gave her verbal directions but did not step in to help. Ao fed all nine cats on her own.

"What do you think? It's going to be like this the whole time."

"It's . . . fine," Ao said, her expression revealing nothing.

She was eager to learn the job quickly so she could do everything on her own.

Misato checked off a sheet clipped to a board, confirming that all the cats had been fed.

"These cats won't be kept for breeding. We socialize them and then sell them. Most of these guys are mixed, so they're quite resilient, but pet stores usually don't want them. The owner is currently looking for new breeding cats. For popular types, you try to emphasize their distinctive traits through breeding. But if you inbreed too much, the cats have more health problems, so we bring in cats from various places to produce healthy and attractive kittens. Does talking about this stuff make you uncomfortable?"

"No," Ao shot back.

Misato laughed.

"Don't worry. We don't do anything unethical here. Quite the opposite, actually. The owner tends to bring in all sorts of cats on a whim, so they end up mixing naturally. But mixed breeds are pretty popular, too. They have lots of personality and aren't expensive, so people buy them. These kittens have beautiful parents, and they're so cute, right? They won't be for sale until the owner returns, though."

Misato's tone was friendly, but her words were focused on profit. As she spoke, she was briskly organizing things around her. She was clearly someone who got things done.

"Now, finally: weaning food. Ms. Torii, will you help me with this?"

As instructed, Ao dissolved the milk powder labeled FOR KITTENS in hot water and stirred it into softened dry food to make a mixture that looked like oatmeal. Ao assumed that they were going to give it to the nine kittens, but Misato brought over a cage from the corner of the room. Inside was another sleeping kitten—the smallest of the bunch.

"This little one just got here. She's only a month old. A breed called Khao Manee."

Ao couldn't speak as she stared at this little creature. She was entirely white, even her round paws and long tail. Only her nose and the insides of her ears were a soft pink. She almost seemed to glow.

The kitten blinked open her eyes—tiny, adorably round eyes.

"White cats are popular, so we're thinking about keeping this one and eventually breeding her with another white one. Doesn't she look a bit like a Japanese bobtail? Cute, right?"

"Her eyes . . ."

"What about them?"

"They're not the same color," murmured Ao in astonishment.

The kitten had eyes of two different shades: one bluish gray, the other ochre.

"She's odd-eyed. Pretty common in white cats. As

she gets older, the blue and yellow will become more distinct. Beautiful, right?"

"So beautiful . . ." Ao replied blankly, her eyes fixed on the dazzling kitten before her.

"We haven't named her yet. We'll only use the name while she's here, but do you want to give her one, Ms. Torii?"

Misato peered into Ao's face.

Ao narrowed her eyes. *We just met. Why is this lady being so intrusive?*

Adults always seemed to get too involved, but they backed off quickly. Her parents and teachers had all tried to meddle, but the moment it seemed they might get scratched, they pulled away.

At any rate, this lady's only pretending to care. This job seems fun, but I'm not here to make friends.

"No, thanks. That sounds like too much responsibility for me."

"Well, okay. I'll come up with a name, like I always do. Hmm, what should I call her?" Misato crossed her arms and tilted her head. "We don't have any other white cats right now, so I guess I'll just name her after her color—Shiro. How's that?"

"That's so obvious . . ."

Ao was exasperated. *A white cat named Shiro—literally, "white."*

For all the effort Misato seemed to have put into picking a name, it was far too simplistic. If there had been another cat of the same color, what then?

"Yup, I've decided on Shiro. You're Ao—blue; and she's Shiro—white. Blue and white. Just like the sky!"

"Is it?" Ao replied icily.

Misato laughed warmly. "It gives a lovely feeling of openness, don't you think? All right, Ao, please help me feed Shiro."

Ao held out a spoonful of softened kibble to the kitten's mouth. Shiro sniffed it a few times before taking a small bite.

"As soon as she begins eating, move the spoon toward her bowl to encourage her to eat by herself."

Ao did as she was told, and Shiro buried her face in the weaning food and milk.

"Her face is all smeared with food . . ."

"Yeah, always a total mess. The area around her mouth will end up looking like a goat's beard, so you'll need to wipe her clean later. Oh, and you have to hold on to her bowl."

The bowl tilted and the bottom rose. Before Ao could

react, it was already too late. Shiro, who had sunk her face too deeply into the bowl, ended up with weaning mash all over her head.

"Oh no!"

"Oh my goodness."

Shiro, wholly absorbed in eating, stepped all over her overturned food, which stained her white fur the color of oatmeal.

"Not good. We'll have to give her a bath later," said Misato.

Ao glanced at the little sink. She couldn't imagine there being a bathtub anywhere here.

She looked at Misato with questioning eyes, and Misato explained, "It's like bathing a baby—difficult to carry out alone, but manageable with two. But unlike a human baby, drying a cat is tricky because—well, they're . . . furry."

It was clear from Misato's strained smile that it was *extremely* tricky.

While communicating wasn't Ao's strong suit, she adapted quickly to new jobs and performed them reasonably well.

But things might not be so simple when cats are involved.

That was the thought that crossed Ao's mind as she watched Shiro sit her butt right in the middle of the gooey food.

Three months had now gone by since Ao's first day at Nakagyō Ni-Nies.

Ao transferred three cats over to the playpen so she could wipe down the cages. In that instant, a fight broke out.

"Hey, stop it! You guys are at it again!"

Ao picked up the fighting cats by their scruffs and pulled them apart. They were the three she always allowed to play together.

They usually got along, but when play fights broke out, Kokubei, the black cat, was always outmatched by the brown cats, Mugi and Choco. Kokubei never fought back, but when things got too rough, he would dodge and dart away so quickly and nimbly that it almost seemed like he might have the upper hand. Still, if it turned into a real fight, one of them could get hurt, so Ao would step in early to break it up.

Cats naturally froze when grabbed by the scruffs of their necks. This instinctive reaction was designed to make it easier for mother cats to carry their kittens in their mouths. So when Ao grabbed their scruffs, it created a relationship beyond just that of caretaker and cat. The cat became the child, and Ao became the mother.

That day, when she grabbed hold of Kokubei, she noticed he had grown heavier. His once-gray eyes had turned golden, like the full moon. The three cats were almost fully grown now, and their fur and eye color had changed as they matured.

It wasn't just their appearance; their personalities were diverse as well. Some had endless energy, some were quick to anger, and others preferred sitting quietly in a corner. Each cat had its own preferences and got along differently with the others.

"Shiman really likes Miiko, doesn't he?" said Misato, smiling as she watched two cats relaxing in their playpen. Shiman, a gray tabby cat, was utterly smitten with Miiko, a calico. The two were the same age, but Shiman was noticeably bigger. He hugged Miiko tightly between two outstretched paws and licked her all over.

"If you keep doing that, Shiman, she's going to—"

Just as Ao uttered those words, Miiko, whose eyes had been closed until then, snapped them open and slapped Shiman on the head. Her quick gesture left Shiman no time to dodge, and the blow hit him squarely on the cheek.

"*See*, she got mad with you again."

Miiko was a beautiful cat—slender, with a well-defined nose. She was a calico with a tail that was slightly bent at the tip. While she was usually calm, her strong-willed nature would show from time to time. Shiman was restless, itching to continue grooming Miiko. He was not easily discouraged—more concerned about keeping Miiko's coat glossy than looking after his own.

Cats are so full of character. And they grow up quickly, thought Ao to herself.

"When is the owner coming back? These kittens have all become adults."

"It's certainly been a while," replied Misato, scooping up clumps of poop from the litter box.

For the past three months, Ao and Misato had been looking after the cats between them. On the one day Ao took off each week, Ms. Asou—the woman who had been put in charge while the owner was away—came in. Ms. Asou rarely came into the office, and when she did, she would leave right away to carry out one household errand or another. Essentially, Misato was the one who monitored the cats' health, and every entry on the feeding log was in her handwriting. She most likely came in every day.

Ao looked forward to going in every day and got along with Misato, who worked quickly and efficiently. But she had caught on to the shadiness of this company as soon as she had begun working for them. They'd basically left Misato, a part-time worker, to handle most of the work, and paid everyone in cash. She doubted they even had the proper licenses or certification required to handle living creatures. The owner, whom she had never once met, was apparently a friend of Ms. Asou's who ran a wide range of businesses around the area.

"The owner's a nice guy, but he's the kind of person who dives headfirst into any idea that pops into his mind," said Misato. "In the past, he's opened a high-end ramen restaurant, an aromatherapy oil store, and a vegan leather shop."

"There's no through line to his ideas," said Ao.

"Exactly. After a while, he always loses interest, so none of those businesses lasted. Still, he apparently wants to expand Ni-Nies. The plan is to bring in more cats, which is why we hired you."

"If we're going to get more cats, I think we should have Ms. Asou come in more often."

"You're pretty blunt, aren't you?" Misato laughed. "Ms. Asou's son is studying for his high school entrance exam, and she's focused on helping him prepare for it. Let's wait until that's finished."

"Doesn't that mean your son's also studying for the entrance exam?"

Ao remembered that Ms. Asou's and Misato's sons were classmates at the same junior high. If one was studying for his entrance exams, the other must be, too.

Misato gave a wry smile. "School life is not for him. My son has hardly been to class since his first year of junior high school. As parents dealing with the same issues, Ms. Asou and I have often cheered each other up. Some people like to lecture me, saying I've spoiled my son, but Ms. Asou said that was definitely not the case. I felt much better after her encouraging words."

This sudden confession from a parent unsettled Ao. Misato's strange concern for her, which had started as soon as Ao began working there, finally made sense. Misato must have seen something of her son in her.

"My son's still holed up at home, but I think he'll eventually start doing something, in his own time. Asou's son managed to go back to school, and he's even motivated to continue his education. It's been tough for me, but Asou introduced me to this job at Ni-Nies and, thanks to her, I've felt much lighter of heart. Cats are such a comfort. They really lift your spirits. Now, let's give them a brush, shall we?"

Cats couldn't resolve household issues, but they could soothe a closed-off heart.

Misato understood the therapeutic effects of cats. She took good care of them without becoming overly attached. Her balance of warmth and distance came from her own self-restraint.

"Shiro, come here for your brushing."

Ao pulled the Khao Manee out of her cage and lifted her to her face. Shiro, who had been four weeks old when Ao first saw her, had grown noticeably larger, and her facial features had sharpened into those of a dignified young cat. Ao had learned that cats, too, have baby teeth that are replaced by permanent teeth. One day, she had noticed something she thought was a tiny piece of plastic in Shiro's poop, and when she had asked Misato about it, she had learned it was Shiro's baby tooth. Misato had said it was rare to find a cat's baby teeth.

Ao learned that Khao Manee was a rare breed. They had short hair, sharp jaws, and slender bodies. Most were solid white, and Shiro, true to her name, was entirely white. Her eyes had changed to a striking blue and yellow. As Ao brushed her, she puzzled over something. Why was her coloring so impossible to ignore? If Shiro were a stray, she would probably be bullied. Cat or human, society rejected those who were different.

"Ao, you look drained. Are you feeling sick?" asked Misato.

Ao shook her head. "I'm okay."

"Really? You're like my son—the type that puts up with everything and says they're fine. Parents take that at face value, and by the time they realize the truth it's already too late. Am I wrong?"

Ao continued to brush, silently wishing Misato would stop projecting her son's difficulties onto her. Misato, like Ao's own mother, tried to understand the source of Ao's problems by expressing what she thought was going on. They were from different generations: Ao's perspective didn't resonate with them and, in turn, their logic felt outdated to her.

Still, Ao and Misato were doing the same job. They were closer in status than Ao was to her teacher or her parents. Even though she found all of this incredibly irritating, Ao responded, "About school—I dropped out because I *didn't* put up with things. I've never been a girly girl, and my name, Ao, is gender-neutral, so wherever I go, there are idiots who make fun of me for that. But I don't ever put up with anything, so whenever something happened at work, I just quit right away. The reason I've stayed here is that I don't see anyone. I don't like people—I like animals."

Ao knew that her parents still thought she had social anxiety disorder, brought on by being bullied at school, but that wasn't true. She just didn't enjoy interacting with people. However, once she stopped forcing herself, the distance between her and others only grew wider.

Misato tilted her head, seemingly confused. "What is there about your name to make fun of? Because it's too hip or something?"

"Not exactly . . ." said Ao. *"Hip"—what a mom thing to say.* "Idiots will make fun of anything."

"Wait, did you not like that I named the cat 'Shiro'? I mean Ao—blue, plus Shiro—white; just like the sky . . . was that cheesy?"

"It's not—no, it is cheesy, but—"

The situation went from being extremely annoying to downright ridiculous. Ao looked away and laughed, and Misato did the same.

"Anyway, don't ever force yourself to say everything's fine. Running away is not always a bad thing."

"Okay."

Ao understood this well. That was why she was there. Adults often tried to console her about her circumstances, but she wasn't upset about it at all. In fact, she liked being in this out-of-the-way space. She wanted to learn more about cats, and maybe, someday, somewhere, she could make use of that knowledge. She was a little surprised to find herself thinking that. It was the first time in a long time that she was looking toward the future.

Shiro grew bored and began swatting at the brush. Her body might be growing into that of an adult, but inside, she was still a kitten. Ao took good care of every cat, but Shiro was special. Because Shiro was the youngest, feeding and litter training took the most effort with her. Maybe that was why she was Ao's favorite.

"You mentioned Shiro wasn't for sale, didn't you?" asked Ao.

"That's right," said Misato. "It all depends on the owner. The cats we have left here are all quite big now. I wonder what will happen to them."

"Grown cats don't sell?"

"They aren't as popular as kittens, but there's always interest. Especially the ones here, because they're well socialized. Folks who can't handle raising kittens or want cats who are used to being around people—there's no shortage of potential buyers."

Misato's tone was matter-of-fact, but Ao wasn't satisfied. She couldn't accept that the owner, who seemed to have no real plan, would decide Shiro's future. Of course, she knew she wasn't in a position to say anything. She needed more experience, and she was determined to acquire it.

After placing Shiro back in her cage, Ao began collecting the trash.

"Do you have anything else to throw out?" she asked Misato. "I'm going to tie up this bag."

"Thanks, I'm good. But, Ao, you really look pale. Are you sure you're not sick?"

"I'm fine."

Cat waste went into the general trash. It was stored in a large airtight container until the next collection day. Ao always made sure to tie the stuffed garbage bags tightly. They were heavy, and taking them out was hard work. By the time she had finished, she was always hot and sweaty.

But that day, a clammy cold sweat came over her. She felt almost light-headed. Still, there was a mountain of tasks she needed to complete. She ignored it and continued to work, only pausing when the doorknob rattled and began to turn. It had been acting up for a while—sometimes refusing to move even when unlocked. Ms. Asou had contacted the building's managing agents, but there had been no response.

When Ao turned the doorknob from the inside, Ms. Asou came bursting in.

"You've been in contact with the managing agents about the door, right, Ms. Asou?" asked Ao.

"What? I don't know anything about that. More importantly, Ms. Hase, we're in trouble. The owner has fled."

"*Fled?*" Misato, in the middle of cat litter cleanup, paused, shovel in hand. "What do you mean?"

"He ran off. Went bankrupt, apparently. I knew he was behind on paying vendors and the rent here, but he kept saying he'd sort it out. But now I can't even pay the two of you. I'm sorry, but you'll have to take any complaints you have to the owner."

Ms. Asou looked pale. Misato shot Ao a worried glance, then turned to Ms. Asou, her voice soft. "Ms.

Asou, where is the owner now? You have his contact information, don't you?"

"I do, but no matter how many times I call, he won't pick up. He's frozen our bank account, so we can't order supplies. No food, no wee-wee pads, nothing!"

"What do you mean?" snapped Ao. Ms. Asou's eyes went wide. "What do you mean, we can't order supplies? With the stock we have now, the food won't last for three days."

"W-well, what am *I* supposed to do?" replied Ms. Asou, clearly annoyed.

The blood rushed to Ao's head. Once that happened, there was no stopping her.

"Ms. Asou, you said yourself that you were in charge while the owner is away! You knew we were behind in our payments. Why haven't you done anything before now?"

"W-why are you speaking to me like that? Who do you think you're talking to?"

"You! I'm talking to you!" shouted Ao. "You could've found someone to take the cats. You could've found the owner and made him take responsibility—there were a ton of things you could have done much sooner. Your family is important, sure, but you should've thought about the cats here as well!"

Ms. Asou's face contorted and she began to tremble. Tears quickly filled her eyes.

"You say that, but I've basically been scammed as well. The owner said he was opening another store, so I put money into the business, and he's run off with it. What am I supposed to tell my husband? And the cats . . . what should we do about them? Ms. Hase, what do we do about the cats?" She sank to the floor.

Ao wanted to click her tongue at her. She didn't know precisely what to do or not do, but the cats would still need the same care tomorrow. Food, brushing, exercise, ear cleaning. Bankruptcy didn't change any of that.

"Ao, you should go home," said Misato.

Ao was taken aback. "What? Why?"

"You shouldn't get involved in this. This was a mistake made by adults. I admit it, I was too lackadaisical myself. We'll ask other businesses to take the cats. If that doesn't work, we'll figure something out ourselves. Isn't that right, Ms. Asou?"

Ms. Asou dropped her head.

Ao felt a surge of anger. She'd thought she could rely

on Misato. After all the work she had put in, when push came to shove, Misato was treating her like a child. Frustrated, she gave her a fierce glare.

"I don't think I trust you," said Ao. "Don't you live in an apartment, Misato? You said they don't allow pets. We have ten cats here. Their food is running out. If we get kicked out of this building, where will these cats go?"

Ao was quivering with anger. She bit down on her trembling lip.

Misato averted her eyes.

"We'll find a place to house them temporarily. If we can't find a solution, we'll have the city or the district help us."

"Are you talking about animal control? What happens to cats that are taken there?" asked Ao.

"If it's just for a short while, I'm sure they'll take them in. Otherwise, we might get in trouble for abandonment or abuse or something."

Ms. Asou, who had been hanging her head all this time, suddenly looked up from where she sat on the floor. "We didn't abuse anything! Why are you blowing this out of proportion? We just ran into business troubles, that's all. We're victims here, too."

"I believe the victims are actually the cats, Ms.

Asou," said Misato, sounding tired. "Listen, Ao, I suggest you don't come back here anymore, okay? You don't want to be arrested by the police, right?"

"Uh, I—"

Ao was suddenly at a loss for words. Ashamed of her own hesitation, she bit down more sharply on her lip. Misato let out a sigh, as if giving up.

"For now, please go home. Whether this place goes bankrupt or not, there's going to be a lot of paperwork. I'll contact you once we know what we're doing."

"Who'll take care of the cats in the meantime?" asked Ao.

"Ms. Asou and I will do that, won't we, Ms. Asou?"

Ms. Asou gave a reluctant nod.

Their logical approach and Ao's bubbling emotions didn't match. Ao left the building unconvinced. She walked so fast that she startled passing pedestrians.

As soon as Ao got home, she withdrew to her room.

What have I done? Why have I backed down like this? she thought.

She had simply walked out of the building, leaving all those cats behind. She buried her head under her blanket. But what could she have done? Even if she had persisted, it would only be a matter of time. The runaway owner wouldn't be caught, and money for cat food wasn't going to fall from the sky. In the end, she had no choice but to leave it to the grown-ups.

She could hear her mother calling her for dinner, but she didn't stir. If she came face-to-face with her now, they would only end up arguing. She knew that if she didn't want to fight, it was best to avoid contact from the start. She didn't want to see anyone or think about anything. The chills she felt were all in her mind. She wasn't weak or soft. *Not one bit*, she told herself.

For the next few days she avoided mealtimes completely, trying her best to steer clear of her family. She had done the same while in high school. Her family would interrogate her constantly about her bad attitude toward her teachers, trying to find answers. In the end, she had dropped out without providing them with any explanation. She didn't regret not having had any answers. And now, she had her own questions.

Why—*why*—had she left the cats behind? Wasn't there anything she could have done?

She kept staring at her phone—still no contact from anyone. Even after searching online, she could find only vague information about what happened when a breeder went bankrupt.

"Bankruptcy . . ."

A thought came to Ao during her research. She walked abruptly out of her room and knocked on her sister's door. Midori came out, her eyes widening at the sight of her sister.

"*Wow*, Ao!"

It was only natural that she would be surprised. This was the first time in years that Ao had approached her sister voluntarily.

Midori's mouth twitched. Ao could sense her hesitation, as if she weren't sure what the expression on her face should be. It had been some time since Ao had really looked at her sister. Five years older, Midori was beautiful and feminine. She had graduated from a national university in Kyoto and worked for a well-known company. Unlike Ao, she was perfect.

Ao averted her eyes.

"Remember the izakaya you used to work at a while ago that went bankrupt? Can you tell me a bit about it?"

"Huh? Izakaya?"

"You said, when you went in one day, the door was locked and you couldn't get in. Did it go bankrupt?"

"*What?* Oh, wait." Midori was flustered. "You mean that job I had in college? It wasn't really a bankruptcy.

More like the owner skipped town in the middle of the night and suddenly shut everything down. No one warned us, so we were all taken by surprise."

"What happened after that? Did someone reopen it?"

"No. They cleared out all the equipment, so it wasn't fit to reopen. I think the creditors probably seized everything. Is something wrong, Ao? I heard from Mom that you're working part-time somewhere around Teramachi. Is something going on there?"

Midori was gentle and caring, kind to everyone, and now, concern was written all over her face.

But Ao had no intention of asking for her help. It was pure misery for her, being constantly compared to the perfect Midori. She didn't blame her sister; it was Ao's own fault for not being able to rise above it. Still, she couldn't look her straight in the eye the way she had when they were kids.

"Nah," Ao replied curtly, and returned to her room. Hearing her sister's story about her old part-time job had not eased Ao's anxiety. Nothing at Nakagyō Ni-Nies was worth taking, except, possibly, the cats.

There was no contact from Nakagyō Ni-Nies the next day either. Ao tried calling Misato but got no answer. *Misato's probably too busy to pick up.* Ao forced herself to believe this, but she had barely slept for days now.

On the third day, Ao found herself once again standing in front of the old, run-down building in Nakagyō Ward. Looking up, she noticed how eternally gloomy it looked. She hadn't thought much of it the first time she came here, but now she wondered how she'd managed to walk in without hesitating.

There had been no word from either of the women, and Ao couldn't wait any longer. She'd come all this way, even though she had caught a bug and was feeling dreadful. She didn't need a thermometer to know she was running a high fever.

She climbed up the stairs to the fifth floor and looked down the empty hallway. The unit at the far end had a window overlooking the street. She remembered discussing with Misato that it would be nice and airy if they had that unit instead.

She turned the doorknob and flinched. It was stiff. *Is it locked?* She broke out into a cold sweat—had they already been evicted? But when she twisted harder, it opened. This building was infuriating. It was miserable enough without the doors being poorly fitted.

As soon as she stepped inside, she noticed that something was off.

The ceiling light was on and Ms. Asou was sitting at a small table. She didn't seem surprised to see Ao and let out a weary sigh.

"I told you not to come back here anymore, Ms. Torii."

"This is *awful*," said Ao, astonished. Her face twisted at the stench.

The cats were in their cages, each one in a terrible condition. The wee-wee pads inside had been torn to shreds, and the interiors were covered in feces and urine.

"Why haven't you been cleaning them? Looks like it's been days . . . Have you even fed them?"

"We're out of food. I just gave them water . . ." Ms. Asou trailed off. Her expression was dark and she began packing documents and a laptop into a cardboard box.

She must be out of her mind.

Ao felt faint with anger.

"Where's Misato? If we're out of food, go and buy some right now!"

"Our bank account is empty. I'm sorry, but you'll need to give up any hope of your pay, too, Ms. Torii. As for Misato, she's disappeared. She hasn't come back since that day."

". . . *What?*"

"My friends took in three of the cats. I gave them the unopened bag of food. They promised to take good care of the cats, so that's a relief. I also gave them the plastic carriers. They belong to the company, so I probably shouldn't have. But what could I do? They said they didn't have anything—no litter boxes, no bowls, nothing. If someone is willing to take in the cats, I want them to have everything they need. But now, there's nothing left—no money or food," said Ms. Asou, closing up the cardboard box.

She was going to run away. Leaving the cats behind.

When Ao peered into the cages, she noticed how strangely the cats were behaving. Some were pacing restlessly, others scratching frantically at the bars; some were just lying there listlessly, and some were just plain dirty.

Ao's mind went blank. The smell was unbearable, but it wouldn't help just to pinch her nose.

After a few moments, she turned and flew out of the

room. Crossing Teramachi Street and Shinkyōgoku Street, she hurried into a discount store that carried pet supplies—a rarity in the busy shopping district. After buying all the cat food she could, she rushed back to the building.

Ms. Asou had vanished. She had left the door unlocked, the lights on, and the cats in their cages.

As soon as the cats caught sight of cat food, they let out a deafening wail—even the adult cats, who rarely made any noise.

"Hang on a moment. Please, just hang on a moment, okay?"

Ao's hands shook as she poured the food into their bowls, scattering some onto the floor. Cleanliness and order could wait. She opened the cage doors one by one.

"Come here, Choco. Here, Miiko. Good kitty."

When she lowered them onto the floor, the cats were shaking. Their fur, once so clean, was soiled and matted.

"Here, Kokubei. You, too."

Ao set the black cat down, and he lumbered over toward the others. Finally, she scooped up Shiro. Shiro felt lighter than before.

"Shiro, you need to eat, too. Don't worry, we have a lot of food."

Shiro mewed softly. Instead of heading directly toward the bowl, she closed her eyes, flattened her ears, and nuzzled forcefully against Ao's leg.

"Shiro, eat. It's okay, you can eat."

She lifted Shiro's now-slender body and placed her nose close to the food bowl. Shiro glanced up and into Ao's eyes with a look of surprise, but then finally began to eat.

Ao had brushed Shiro almost every day. She had loved her white fur, and to maintain her beauty she had groomed Shiro more carefully than the others. That was why, even though Shiro's stomach was empty, she wanted to be groomed.

Only humans thought white fur was beautiful. Out in the wild, a cat like this would stand out too much to survive.

"Shiro . . ."

The stench was overwhelming. The single fan in the back of the room wasn't enough to drive out the smell. This sealed-off space was their whole world. These cats couldn't survive outside it.

Ao had trusted the adults, and they had betrayed her. Misato and Ms. Asou had both run away. But she couldn't fix this on her own.

She needed to ask for help.

Someone reliable.

With trembling hands, Ao pulled out her phone. She looked up the Kyoto animal control website, but she couldn't figure out which office had jurisdiction over their area. She dialed a number anyway, and while it rang, anxious thoughts darted through her head. Would they ask her for her name? She wasn't a minor, but would they contact her family? She didn't even know the owner's name.

The line connected, and someone on the other end was burbling something she couldn't make out. She had no clue which department she had reached or to whom she should be transferred.

Who would take responsibility? What if they told her to take in all the cats? She couldn't possibly take them home. If she were to . . .

Ao glanced at Shiro. She was eating alongside the other cats. Ao's lips quivered. She had begun to weep.

She grasped her phone tightly with both hands. "There are cats trapped in a room," she said. She didn't know the name of the street where this building was. "Rokkaku or Takoyakushi Street in . . . Nakagyō Ward. On the fifth floor of a narrow building. Please help them."

Someone was speaking on the other end. Ao was afraid. She wished she hadn't called from her own phone. If there were only one cat, she could have brought it home. Her parents would complain, of course, but she could have handled just one.

Then how about one more cat?

Would it be okay if it were a docile one? If they were low-maintenance, how many could she take? If one cat was okay, wouldn't two or three be fine, too?

At the very least, just Shiro . . .

She instantly shook off those thoughts. She was well aware of the work that went into caring for a cat.

Ao hung up the phone. She had called animal control. For now, she didn't know what else she could do.

She would come again tomorrow, she thought. Even if no one came to help, she would continue coming to take care of them.

She wiped away her tears and got down to work, giving the cats water and cleaning up their excrement. By the time she had put each cat back into its cage, she was drenched in sweat and her hands were shaking.

The cats were watching her from their cages. Their eyes asked: *Why won't you play with us? Why won't you brush us? How about trimming our claws?*

Ao fled the room, ran down the stairs and out of the building. She couldn't choose among the cats. She couldn't take only Shiro.

Her meager savings would run out quickly. When she got home, she would talk to her parents and ask for advice. It might not be possible for them to take in every cat, but she would plead with them to consider paying for their food until each one found a home.

Her body felt heavy, and getting onto the bus home, she had to hold the handrail. As soon as she took her seat, her eyelids grew heavy.

"Hey, are you okay?" asked a distant voice. It was a woman.

Her body swayed with the bus's movements. Someone was making a fuss around her, but Ao, her eyes shut, had been sucked into darkness.

When she regained consciousness, a dreadful headache and nausea made it impossible for her to think. It wasn't until five days after she had collapsed on the bus that she had been able to get up on her own again. Severe pneumonia had led to septic shock, knocking her out cold as her blood pressure crashed. Still, somehow, there had been no damage to her organs.

Even while she was in a daze, she hadn't forgotten about the cats she had left behind. She thought she had told everyone about that building, but in reality it had come out as delirious ramblings that neither her parents nor the nurses had been able to understand. Her phone had died, so even if someone had tried to call her, the call wouldn't have gone through. She had tried calling Misato and Ms. Asou, but neither of them had answered.

What was the situation like now? Her strength had not returned, and her legs shook. Still, Ao slipped out of the hospital.

As she swayed, standing in the bus, she prayed into her clenched fist that everything would be okay. Misato and Ms. Asou were not bad people. They had to realize what would happen to the cats if they were abandoned for days. And she had also called animal control. Surely, they would have rescued them. It was definitely going to be okay. It couldn't *not* be. That would be unimaginable. That would be unforgivable.

She got off the bus on a main road and turned down a narrow alley. People often said that Kyoto's streets were laid out like a grid, but in fact they were not that straightforward. The small shops that filled the gaps between bigger buildings didn't serve as landmarks, and narrow paths you could barely call streets appeared out of nowhere. They were difficult to enter and even harder to find. The Nakagyō Building was even one of the easier ones to locate. It was set slightly back from the main road, but at least it faced it.

As always, the door was wide open, revealing the hallway that led all the way to the back of the building. Ao peered in. Nothing had changed. There was no barrier of yellow tape or posters; there was no trace of any disturbance at all. On the street, there was not a single pedestrian in sight. It was as if time had stopped.

Feeling anxious and unsteady on her feet, she went down the corridor toward the staircase. The walls in this building were unusually thick, and their solidity prevented any sound from traveling through them. Still, she had usually been able to hear the cats meowing when she got near. As she climbed the stairs to the fifth floor, she wondered how they had never had any complaints.

She could not hear the meows now.

"Ugh . . ."

Ao bit down on her lip and swallowed the sobs that

threatened to erupt. Her feet stopped on the fourth-floor landing. The smell had reached this far. Had animal control not come? In the end, there was no one she could depend on. Gritting her teeth, she despaired that no one had come to help.

No, that's not right. Why didn't I *come, even if I had to crawl to get here?*

Should she have at least taken Shiro home with her? She could have saved one cat. Even if it meant abandoning all the other cats, was that what she should have done?

Her knees shook violently. She was scared. She didn't want to see.

Still, she put one foot in front of the other until she was standing in front of the unit. The stench was unbearable. She steeled herself and grabbed the doorknob. She squeezed both eyes shut and turned.

The door wouldn't budge.

It was locked.

"Wh-why?"

She pounded frantically on the metal door, but only the banging echoed through the hallway.

The door had been unlocked when she was here before. Ms. Asou and Misato each had a key. They might have abandoned the cats, but she never imagined they would lock them in.

"Oh god, what do I do?"

The door was thick. There was no way she could break it down.

The window? Could she climb in from the neighboring building? No, that was too dangerous. She looked around, half in a panic. The other units on this floor were empty. If she ventured downstairs and knocked on every door, she might find someone.

On trembling legs, she made her way down the stairs and out onto the street. She could see a TENANTS WANTED sign stuck to the inside of a window on the fifth floor. The sign listed the managing agent's telephone number. Looking more carefully, she could also make out an old-fashioned sign on the front wall that read NAKAGYŌ BUILDING.

She now had the managing agent's contact number, but with a start she realized they were very likely totally behind on the rent. Would it be odd for an employee of the vanished tenant to ask the management to unlock the door? They might reject her outright, saying the cats were none of her business.

Then an idea came to her. She decided instead to call

as a "concerned neighbor," complaining about a foul stench in the building. She didn't mention her name, and insisted the smell was so bad they had to come right away. She emphasized this several times before hanging up.

Then she crossed over the street and crouched low. She stayed perfectly still, keeping her eyes fixed on the building's entrance. She should have done this a long time ago, should have acted when Ms. Asou made a fuss about the owner fleeing. She, who had looked away because she was afraid, was just as much to blame.

She had no idea how long she had been waiting. It was starting to grow dark, and lights were turning on. Unable to hold on any longer, she took out her phone to look for someone else who could help, searching for groups in the Nakagyō Ward area that took in cats. Several results appeared. She examined one of the options.

"At the City Cat Rescue Center, we host monthly cat adoption fairs . . . We connect our rescues with their forever homes . . ."

It's located on the edge of Kyoto but still well within the city, so they might help.

Ao dialed the number. She called several times, but no one answered. Just when she thought this place was no good either and was about to hang up, the line connected.

"Hello, City Cat Rescue Center." The voice belonged to a man—high-pitched, slightly nasal, and rather unenthusiastic.

"Um."

This was it. If they wouldn't help, she'd need to contact the police.

"Several cats have been locked up in a room for days. In a building in Nakagyō Ward, around Rokkaku and Takoyakushi Street . . ."

Shoot, she still didn't know the address. She should have checked her phone for her location. How could she be so stupid?

Any distinguishing features . . .

She had gone down the wrong street once. The episode remained in her memory.

"It's called the Nakagyō Building—the very top floor of a narrow five-story building. Second unit from the end. Um, it's close to Teramachi. It's quite a bit in from Karasuma, and there's a clinic in an old town house just behind it."

There was a brief silence before the voice replied, curt and to the point. "Do you mean Dr. Kokoro's clinic?"

"What? I-I'm not sure."

"So somewhere behind Suda Animal Clinic in Nakagyō Ward, right? We'll head over right away."

The call ended. It was the greatest sense of urgency she had heard from anyone yet.

Ao stayed low, nestled near a wall with her arms wrapped around her legs. After a while, she heard the sound of an engine and raised her head. A car pulled up in front of the building. It had the leasing company's corporate sticker on its side. A middle-aged man wearing a tie emerged and walked into the building. Ao looked on, barely breathing.

Someone from the managing agents. *Maybe he'll unlock the door, look around, and come out unfazed by what he's seen.* But Ao's faint hope vanished in an instant when the man came flying out, pale and shaken, frantically dialing a number on his phone. She couldn't hear what he was saying as he climbed back into the car, but his ashen face had said enough. What he'd seen, Ao couldn't begin to guess.

Another vehicle arrived. A white delivery van. The door opened and a man stepped out.

Ao had a gut feeling that this was the guy from the rescue center. The man moved quickly, popping open the back and hauling out a big bag, hoisting it onto his shoulder. As he was about to walk into the building, the man in the other car got out.

"Hey! Are you the person who called us about the smell?"

"No, I—" The guy from the rescue center looked surprised, but his expression quickly turned serious. "We received a report that there are cats trapped in a unit on the fifth floor of this building, and I'm here to save them. Are you the superintendent?"

"I'm from the managing agents, but the cats are beyond the point of saving . . ."

For a moment, the man from the rescue center turned his face away, as if in pain. But he quickly composed himself. "Please call Dr. Kokoro Suda from the clinic behind this building. If you tell him Kajiwara is asking for him, he'll understand."

He turned and ran inside the building. The other man appeared shaken. He took off down the street. Within a few minutes, he reappeared, accompanied by an older man in a white lab coat and plastic sandals and with wildly disheveled hair. Together, they disappeared inside the building.

Only Ao remained outside, unable to do anything but silently observe from her hiding place.

After a while, something resembling a wail could be heard coming from inside the building. Ao froze. It was the cry of a cat, a low, pained sound. The man from the rescue center emerged, holding a pet carrier. A jet-black cat was thrashing wildly inside it.

"Kokubei," she whispered.

Tears filled her eyes.

Next, the man from the managing agents came out, holding another pet carrier. Ao could make out a calico lying inside.

"Miiko."

He was followed by the man in a white lab coat, who also held a carrier.

"Kajiwara—your arm—you have to go to the hospital," said the man in the white lab coat.

"I'll go later. This comes first. Let's transport them by car."

His arm looked bloody, but he seemed not to care. He opened the back of his van and climbed inside. Working with the man from the managing agents, they loaded up the van with pet carriers. They lugged out carriers from the building, emerging twice more, then again. Passersby gathered amid the commotion, but no one stepped forward to help.

The man in the white coat came out of the building carrying yet another carrier. Who knew how many trips he had made up to the fifth floor. He was breathing heavily, clearly out of breath.

"This is the last one. We'll find a way to save it somehow. Hang in there, kitty!" he said as he handed the carrier to the rescue worker.

For just a moment, Ao caught a glimpse inside the carrier.

Shiro's body was no longer pure white.

"Shiro, Shiro, Shiro . . ."

Her heart was about to shatter. She couldn't breathe.

The man from the rescue center got into the driver's seat, and with the man in the lab coat in the passenger seat, the van pulled away. The van left, with only the managing agent still there, rooted to the spot.

"My goodness. What cruelty. It was like a crime scene."

Letting out a theatrically loud sigh, he got into his car, then made another phone call.

Silence returned to the street, as if nothing had happened. Not a soul in sight, and the building's entrance gaped open, as always. Everything looked so unchanged that Ao could have convinced herself the cats were still up on the fifth floor, waiting for her.

But they weren't. They were gone. What she'd witnessed had been real. The fifth floor held no life anymore.

And she was to blame.

She was completely dried out; there were no tears left. Ao walked away.

"You're Ao, aren't you?" asked the woman who had just finished paying at the register.

Ao raised her eyes. She'd been keeping them low, pretending not to notice the woman staring at her. Her face looked familiar.

"I'm Emiri. You might not remember me. We were in junior high school together. Emiri Koga."

"Oh," Ao replied vacantly.

She felt a wave of nostalgia at the sight of Emiri's unchanged smile. They had been in the same class in the second year of junior high and would often get excited about their favorite manga. She was a friendly girl—even after they were separated into different classes, she always waved whenever they bumped into each other. Even now, she was just as carefree, as if no time had passed at all.

"Long time no see!" said Emiri. "I'm studying at a college in Shiga Prefecture, and I come to this diner sometimes. I've never noticed you working here, though."

"I usually work in the kitchen," Ao mumbled, then looked away.

She had been working here part-time for six months, but she seldom worked front of house. There were a ton of customers, and there were many other servers. How unlucky she was to coincidentally end up handling the bill for someone she knew, a former classmate, when she had intentionally chosen this spot along the Kosei train line in Shiga Prefecture to avoid running into people from her hometown.

Maybe she didn't notice Ao's awkwardness, or she simply understood that Ao had always been unfriendly, but Emiri seemed happy.

"Do you use social media? Give me your contact information."

"I only browse other people's accounts."

Ao's vague response didn't seem to register as a refusal, and Emiri handed Ao her phone. It seemed Emiri's companion was waiting for her at the entrance, and that concerned Ao, too.

Reluctantly, Ao took out her phone and they exchanged contact information. It was only for now, anyway. She didn't keep in touch with anyone for long.

"It's amazing that our manga is still going," said Emiri brightly. "Ao, are you still a superfan of the same character?"

"Y-yeah."

"Me, too."

Emiri laughed just as she had in junior high, then left.

Ao felt restless. Even as she silently cleaned the dining room and worked in the kitchen, she remained agitated. A mix of ticklishness and discomfort swirled inside her.

The part-time jobs she juggled included picking parts in a factory and cleaning hotel rooms—each requiring minimal human contact. Even at this restaurant, she typically prepared food and washed dishes, rarely appearing before customers.

As she headed to the staff break room in the back, Matsuo, another part-timer, called out to her from behind her.

"Ms. Torii, I'm sorry to make you work front of house all of a sudden. You really saved me."

She put her hands together in gratitude. Her arm was wrapped in bandages and gauze.

Matsuo, a woman in her forties, usually worked in the dining room. She was cheerful, always welcoming guests with a bright smile and a loud greeting. She was so amiable that she even chatted with the unsociable Ao.

Matsuo had shown up for her shift today with a large bandage on her forehead. She'd begged Ao to cover for her because she couldn't face customers looking like that. Before Ao knew it, she had found herself working front of house. Thanks to that, she had run into a former classmate and ended up in an uncomfortable situation.

The two of them entered the break room. There was no one else there. Ao, as always, sat in the corner by herself, killing time on her phone. Today, Matsuo sat down opposite her. She let out a loud sigh, as if she wanted to talk.

"I bet everyone's suspicious about how I got my injuries. No matter how many times I explain what happened, I get awkward smiles. But I promise it's nothing dodgy. A cat attacked me. Here, look!"

She peeled back the gauze, revealing several red scratch marks.

Ao cringed at the sight of them.

"You showed me this morning already."

"Did I? I wonder if it'll scar. My arm is one thing, but my forehead—it's too much! We found the chonky cat we had for a few days while we were barbecuing by Lake Biwa. She was huge, but so gentle. You could rub her belly all you wanted. She was more like a cushion than a cat. But this new one is entirely different. Have you ever owned a cat, Ms. Torii?"

"I, um . . ." Ao turned away. "Haven't."

Almost three years had passed since that day when she had watched the pet carriers being driven off. Ao had felt her anger, which had nowhere to go, threatening to turn on her family, so she had left home shortly afterward. Truth was, things had been strained with her parents long before she dropped out of high school. If anything, she'd felt relieved—finally, she had a reason to put some space between them.

She lived alone now, her days filled with back-to-back part-time jobs. At work, she kept things strictly professional, never sharing anything personal, and this diner was no exception. She hadn't even known Matsuo had a cat until she'd asked Ao to cover her shift.

"The one we have right now is called Fuku-chan. She was apparently a stray until recently, so she's very wary. I think Chonky Cat's gentleness was partly down to her personality, but I think her owner also taught her that humans are kind. Fuku-chan doesn't trust humans. Just when I thought we'd become a little closer . . . she lashed out and scratched my forehead. Still, I feel like if I'd had more time, we could have become better friends. It feels sad to think that tomorrow is our last day together—I feel like I've done something unfair to Fuku-chan. I get the feeling she wants to stay with us."

Matsuo looked dejected, her usual brightness gone.

Ao was puzzled. "What do you mean, tomorrow is your last day together?"

"I'm going over tomorrow to give her back. I got Fuku-chan from a place where they loaned her to me for ten days. You grew up in Kyoto, right? Kyoto addresses are really difficult to work out. Like north of Fuyacho Street, or south of Tominokoji Street, or west of Rokkaku Street, or east of Takoyakushi Street. I had a hard time finding it. It was in this narrow building that I almost walked right past."

Ao felt a nasty chill run down her back.

She recognized the street names. It was probably close to *that* place. But there were plenty of narrow buildings in the area. They all looked similar. Ao remained silent.

"It's an old building with no elevator—in this day and age!"

There were more old buildings than new ones in that neighborhood.

"And it's on the fifth floor! I'm depressed just thinking about climbing all those stairs tomorrow with Fuku-chan in tow."

Ao's sense of dread was growing.

Fifth floor of a building. Given a cat to look after?

". . . Is it in the second unit from the end?"

"Oh! Do you know it?"

"Maybe." She let out a slow breath.

She was feeling rattled. That day when the cats had been taken away in that van, she had thought that was the end of it.

But perhaps Nakagyō Ni-Nies was not gone.

"It's a really odd place. I was told about it by an old man who said that a cat that looks just like Chonky Cat was 'applied' to him."

"Do they raise cats in that unit?"

"I don't know if they raise them, but there are cats there. They brought Fuku-chan out from behind a curtain."

"There are cats there . . ." mumbled Ao.

She bit her lip. It had to be a coincidence. It just so happened that in the same unit, someone else was raising cats. And for reasons that were unclear.

Matsuo likely hadn't a clue about what had happened in that unit—and if she had, she'd have kept her distance. Telling her now would be nothing short of meddling, and Ao knew that the fact she cared at all was more than a bit hypocritical.

She stroked the pendant at her neck—a small stainless-steel capsule holding Shiro's baby tooth. She wore it as a constant reminder to herself. Each time her fingers found it, her breath caught in her chest.

This was not the moment to run away. It felt like Shiro was telling her that.

"Are you going to that building tomorrow, Ms. Matsuo?"

"Yes. I'm sad about it, but I have to go and return her."

"May I come with you?"

"Come with me? Why?"

"I might know the people who keep cats there, so I'd like to see them. See how they're doing now."

It had all happened three years ago. Even if the cats had been saved, they would be long gone from that building by now. And even with the one-in-a-million chance that they were still there, they certainly wouldn't be waiting for Ao, the person who had failed them.

Still, she needed to see for herself to confirm that not a single one of those cats had been left behind.

Ao got off at the Sanjō subway stop and waited aboveground on the Sanjō Ōhashi Bridge until Matsuo turned up.

She arrived carrying a pet carrier, flanked by two young children—a boy who looked to be in early elementary school, and a girl who was even younger. Both were clutching the hem of her coat.

"Sorry, the kids insisted on coming. My son is Haruma, and this is Yua. Kids, this lady is Mom's friend, Ao Torii. Say hello."

The two children bowed in unison. Ao stood frozen. She had known Matsuo was bringing Fuku-chan, the cat, but she hadn't expected the kids. She was not good with kids.

The kids positioned themselves on either side of Ao.

Why are they coming over to me? Ao felt flustered.

Matsuo, carrying the cat carrier with some effort, strolled ahead, while the children chatted with Ao, vying for her attention.

"I know how to write 'Fuku-chan' in kanji characters. Wanna see?" asked Haruma.

"I know, too!" exclaimed Yua. "I also drew a picture of Fuku-chan. Wanna see?"

"You only know how to write it in hiragana, Yua. I can write it in kanji. Want me to show you?"

"I'll show you mine, too! Wanna see?"

It was unclear what the two wanted from her. Ao was paying close attention to avoid their having a fall or an accident. She didn't appreciate their tugging on the edge of her clothing. Her sleeves were stretching. But she would rather that than lose sight of them. The three walked in a line, following Matsuo.

They entered Teramachi Street from Kyogoku Street,

and after walking down the arcade for a while, they turned onto Rokkaku Street.

Ah, just as I thought. She had expected it, but she still felt disappointed. Matsuo was heading toward the Nakagyō Building on Fuyacho Street. The building had not changed at all—tall, narrow, old-fashioned. The only differences were that there was no longer a TENANTS WANTED sign in the top-floor window and the blinds were down. It seemed the unit facing the street had been rented.

Matsuo tilted her head.

"How odd. Was it here? I thought it was at the end of an alley."

She peered into the entrance, looking perplexed.

The door gaped open just as before.

Matsuo turned around before going in.

"Haruma, Yua, I'm going to give Fuku-chan back now. You two stay with Ao down here, okay?"

The kids exchanged glances, Ao standing between them.

"I'm going with you," said Haruma.

"Me, too. I'm going to say bye-bye to Fuku-chan," said Yua.

"I'm coming, too," said Ao.

As the four of them walked into the building, the narrow hallway felt tight. The children were quicker going up the stairs—they climbed ahead in no time. Partway up, Ao turned around. Matsuo was on the third floor, out of breath.

"I can hold the carrier, Matsuo."

"Really? Thank you." Matsuo was massaging her lower back.

Through the mesh panel of the door, Ao could see the cat inside—a mixed breed with white-tipped ears and a youthful-looking face.

"How old is this cat?"

"According to the instruction leaflet, it's eight months old."

An eight-month-old cat. The trio of friends who were always playing together had been around the same age, too, if she remembered correctly.

The fifth floor had not changed at all. The paint on every door was chipped. There was not a person in sight; all was quiet. No smell. No meows.

Ao stood in front of the second unit from the end with the cat carrier in her arms. She was afraid to open the door, unsure of what might be behind it.

"I'll open the door for you," said Yua, grabbing the doorknob.

Then Haruma placed his hand on top of hers.

"I'll open it."

"No, I will!"

"I will!"

While the two fought over the doorknob, a voice sounded from the end of the hallway.

"Are you here for a viewing, by chance?"

Ao turned and saw a young man on the stairs approaching them with a lively smile.

"Perfect timing. I just showed the unit to someone else. Great property, right? It's a little old, but the location is excellent, and it's very affordable, considering its condition. The wallpaper and flooring have been replaced and look beautiful. Please, come in."

The man was all smiles as he opened the door for the children.

Ao's field of vision suddenly brightened. Beyond the door was an empty room. A large window faced them and the light pouring in bounced off the white walls and floor. The man handed Matsuo and Ao his business card.

Ao recognized the leasing agency. Three years ago,

she had called the company and a car bearing this company's logo had come.

This man was younger than the agent who had handled things back then. With a friendly smile, he opened the north-facing window.

"You get light from this side window, and the view is great, too. The last person I showed this space to is considering it, so if you're interested, you'll need to move fast."

Finding the empty room a novelty, the two kids were excited. Ao looked around. It felt as if she were visiting this place for the first time. Now completely empty, the space felt so much larger.

Matsuo stood in the middle of the room, dazed.

"What happened? There was a reception window here and a chair here. I also went into an examination room. I spoke to a weird doctor. And I was prescribed Fuku-chan. The doctor gave him to me for ten days, so I came back, like I was supposed to."

Ao didn't think Matsuo was lying. As far as she was concerned, such an interaction had taken place. What mattered more than pressing for details or ironing out inconsistencies was the present moment. There was an actual cat currently sitting in the carrier, a cat whose destiny had been left in the hands of humans.

Ao passed the carrier over to Matsuo.

"Here. If today's the return day, she's still your cat."

"Well, yes, that's true. She's still our cat."

Matsuo took the carrier and peeked in through the mesh.

"What should we do, Fuku-chan? You don't have anywhere to go back to."

"Mommy." Yua tugged on Matsuo's sleeve. "I want to go home."

"Bored already? Give me a second. Mommy's trying to figure something out."

"I want to go home with Fuku-chan."

Yua looked up at Matsuo. Then Haruma tugged at her other sleeve.

"Me, too, Mommy. Let's take Fuku-chan home."

Just as they had when they arrived, the three humans and one cat stood in a line. Matsuo looked dumbfounded.

"So what do you think? If you'd like, we can provisionally hold this unit for you," said the smiling agent.

There was nothing suspicious about the agent or the

unit itself. However, what worried Ao was whether something similar to what she had experienced here could happen again.

"Are animals allowed in this building?"

"Animals? Let me see." The agent checked his tablet. "Ah, per the wishes of the landlord, no animals are allowed in any of the units."

That was to be expected. It was strange that animals had been allowed in an office building. That situation had been abnormal.

Ao fingered the capsule that hung from her necklace. She didn't know when things had started to go wrong. But now, she could make things right.

"Matsuo, this cat and the kids are not meant to be here."

". . . Yeah? I guess you're right."

Matsuo lowered her eyes to the carrier in Ao's arms, then looked between the two children now flanking her.

"Let's go home with Fuku-chan, Haruma and Yua."

The family filed out of the room.

The agent looked puzzled. "Hey! You're leaving already? Are you interested in this unit?"

"No," called Matsuo.

Ao followed soon after. A loud metallic clang echoed

behind her. Even though she now knew the place was empty, she felt unsettled. She should have felt relieved, but what was this hollow emptiness she felt inside her?

There's nothing here anymore. They're really gone.

Matsuo and the children were waiting for her downstairs when she arrived, tears in her eyes.

Haruma approached her and grinned. "Do you want me to hold your hand?"

"How cheeky of you!" Ao replied.

She wiped away the tears and shot him a playful glare. Then she walked out of the building, hand in hand with the children.

After crossing Sanjō Ōhashi Bridge and nearing the stairs that descended into the subway stop, she noticed it. She grabbed at her chest, but there was nothing there.

Ao froze.

"What's wrong, Ms. Torii?" asked Matsuo.

"Um, my . . ." She was going to say her necklace was missing, but she didn't want to worry them. "I just remembered I need to buy something. I'm going to stop at a store."

"Oh, okay. I'm glad you came with us today—thank you. Haruma, Yua, say good-bye."

"Bye-bye." The two waved in unison.

She saw Matsuo and her kids off, then turned back the way she had come, to search for the silver chain.

She remembered feeling the necklace on the fifth floor of that building. She swept her eyes over every corner of the sidewalk as she walked down Kyogoku Street and Teramachi Street before turning onto Rokkaku Street. The building was on Fuyacho Street. To return so quickly after she'd thought she'd never go back again—she was frustrated by her own foolishness.

A few moments passed. Then, "Wait—what?" she said.

Because she had been looking only at the ground, she had already walked past the building. She turned back in frustration. There was no sign of the necklace. Had she dropped it inside the building?

Before she knew it, she was at the intersection again.

"Wait, I just walked this way . . . what's going on?"

Identical buildings, identical houses. She was going around in circles. Was it her sense of direction that was off—or was it her? She was starting to lose track of which street she was on.

She came to a stop. Beside her stretched a dark alley. At the end was a faint outline of a building, its door wide open.

Nakagyō Building. Puzzled, Ao entered the building. Narrow hallway. Stairs in the back. The nameplates on the doors looked somewhat familiar. On the fifth floor, she found the heavy, peeling metal door, just as she remembered it.

Her necklace was not in the hallway. Ao felt her stomach drop with disappointment. She wanted to go inside the unit to check, but the leasing agent had likely locked it before leaving. Still, she grasped the doorknob. It couldn't hurt to—

Click. The doorknob turned.

"It's open . . ."

The door was unlocked. Whether from warping or from wear, it opened a little, but was very heavy.

She felt a surge of anger. That smiling agent—he had made it look like the door opened easily, but in reality, they hadn't fixed the door fitting. She grabbed the doorknob with both hands and pushed with all her strength.

The door opened.

Inside was no longer a white, empty room. There was no window.

There was something that looked like a reception window. As Ao stood in a daze, she heard the patter of slippers as a nurse appeared.

"Ms. Torii? We've been waiting for you."

She was a pale woman in her mid-twenties. Her eyes gestured for Ao to come in, but Ao couldn't move from the spot.

"Um, this place . . ."

"You have an appointment, don't you? Please take a seat in the chair and wait."

"I don't have an appointment. I just came to look for the necklace I lost."

"If you mean the silver necklace, Dr. Nikké was playing with it just now. I hope it's not broken. We've been waiting for you."

A human playing with a necklace?

Ao shook her head in disbelief.

"Please take a seat," said the nurse curtly.

Still confused, Ao stepped inside. The interior was completely different from before; it was a simple waiting room. She sat in the armchair.

If this was a dream, when had it begun?

Her fingers reflexively went to her chest, but there was still no necklace there, though it was apparently somewhere in this peculiar space. If it was broken, whom could she hold responsible?

From behind the door next to the chair, a male voice called out.

"Please come in, Ms. Torii."

It wasn't a matter of being scared or mystified—she was beyond that now. Ao pushed open the door. Inside was a small examination room with a single desk and a computer. A doctor in a white coat was sitting there.

"We've been waiting for you, Ms. Torii. I'm so glad you didn't forget to come."

He was a young man, likely in his early thirties, with a plain, unremarkable face you might see anywhere.

"The grapevine can be helpful. Thanks to it spreading absolutely everywhere, it finally reached even you. I did what I could, too—singing, dancing, all sorts of things. But in the end, it wasn't me who got you to come. So, what brings you in today?"

The doctor smiled gently.

She still didn't understand what was going on. Even if this were a dream, there was one thing she wanted to say. She gave him a glare.

"Give me back my necklace."

"Understood." The doctor nodded. "We'll prescribe you a cat." He spun around in his chair and called out toward the back of the room, "Chitose! Please bring the cat."

The nurse emerged from between the curtains, a simple plastic crate in her arms. She looked down at the doctor and said coldly, "Dr. Nikké, isn't this cat a bit too intense for Ms. Torii?"

"It'll be fine. Bitter medicine is the best medicine. The best cats are bitter—that's why they're so effective. You're so thoughtful, Chitose."

"It's just that you are utterly thoughtless," she responded, setting the crate on the desk before leaving, looking like she couldn't care less.

Ao couldn't understand the meaning of the exchange she had just witnessed, but apparently, there was a cat inside the crate. They were raising cats here again. Ao glared intensely at the doctor.

"Are you aware that, a few years ago, many cats suffered right here in this room? This place is not suitable for raising animals. Cats shouldn't be here."

"It's true—no one is bound to this place anymore. Everyone's free now. Once our last scheduled patient is healed, we can finally close up shop. So, what do you say? Isn't it time you let go of your anger?" said the doctor gently.

Let go of my anger?

Ao was momentarily stunned. She wasn't angry. She was composed and acting appropriately. Why did people always say that to her just because she wasn't friendly all the time?

"You know nothing about me." Frustration welled up inside her, and she heard her voice grow shrill. "I'm just acting normally, for goodness' sake. I am *not* angry, and I am *not* sulking. So why do people keep asking me if I'm angry? I'm tired of being compared to my sister."

After letting it all out, she suddenly realized what she had done. She had misdirected her anger. This doctor had nothing to do with her discontent. Bitterly, she shut her mouth.

The doctor was unperturbed. He was even smiling a little.

"There's anger inside of you. There's anger inside of me, too. We all need it to survive. But being belligerent all the time is not okay. The 'wanna fight?' pose of a cat—the arched back and puffed tail—can sometimes spark pointless conflict. It might look funny, but it can also come across as a 'bring it on' kind of attitude, as if you're always ready to fight."

The doctor nodded to himself.

Ao frowned, unsure of what the doctor meant.

"What are you talking about?"

"Oh, the 'wanna fight?' pose—do you not know it? Shall I show you?"

The doctor began to rise from his chair. Ao shrank back.

"Aah. No, thank you. I know what it is."

"You want to line your shoulders with your head. Wonder if my head . . . maybe not. That hurts." The doctor held his head in his hands and seemed to actually be trying to pull it off his neck. "No good. Maybe I can dislocate my shoulders. If I force it, I might just manage it."

"That's enough." The grotesque idea made Ao's cheek twitch. "Please stop."

"Oh, all right."

The doctor looked disappointed as he retook his seat.

The "wanna fight?" pose was a stance cats assumed—back arched into a small mound, face tucked into their contracted body. They moved sideways with their outstretched limbs, making for a comical sight. But they adopted this posture when they were on alert or felt threatened, so it probably wasn't fun for the cat. *And he wanted to show me* that? Ao's suspicions grew.

The doctor was grinning foolishly. "Anyway, everyone has the pose . . . no, I mean, anger within them. But I want you to understand that anger can hurt you, too. That's why this cat is perfect for you. Like you, she also carries anger within her."

The doctor turned the crate so the mesh panel door faced Ao.

There was a white cat inside.

Her eyes were gold and blue. In the shadows, her pupils narrowed to sharp lines, thin as knives. Ao gasped.

"Shiro . . ."

"Beautiful, right? Pure white cats have a hard time surviving in the wild. Perhaps humans love them because they are destined to live difficult lives. Please take this cat for five days. I'll write you a prescription, so do pick up what you need at reception. First, take this cat, and then we can start making various changes. You'll be fine. You came here on your own two feet—that alone is a massive first step."

The cat crouched low in the carrier and glared at her. She was a short-haired, pure white cat with a taut face. A tense wariness radiated from her.

Pure white Shiro. Ao—blue, and Shiro—white. Just like the sky. It was Misato, whom Ao had worked with here, who had said that there was a lovely feeling of openness to their names. The memory slightly calmed her. She tore her eyes away from the cat and turned back to the doctor.

"I didn't come here because I wanted to. I was just accompanying someone."

"Oh, is that so?" The doctor cocked his head, seeming puzzled. "But you opened the door yourself, didn't you?"

"That's because I was looking for the necklace. Maybe the door doesn't fit right, but it was pretty heavy," she said in a pointed tone.

The doctor's eyes widened.

"Oh my, oh my, oh my. Well, well, *well*."

What's with the "oh mys"? Ao's temper began to flare at his mockery, and she frowned. Yet the doctor remained nonchalant.

"Is that *so*? Maybe it was a bit early for you to come here, Ms. Torii. But whims are whims, yet also not whims. Things that seem trivial can have meaning, and meaningful things can be trivial. If there's something important to you right now, let's take care of that first—even if you change your mind tomorrow."

He pushed the carrier toward Ao. Ao shrank back.

"The cat—I can't."

"Haha! Don't lie!"

"I'm not lying. I just can't."

The doctor laughed. "You heard her say it just now: I'm utterly thoughtless! If you find that you absolutely can't, please return the cat even if you're still partway through the prescription. But this one will have a hard time out in the world. So, she'll be loved by humans, and she'll encounter suffering. Love doesn't always guarantee happiness—that's true not just for cats. Now, take care."

The cat, her ears pinned back, stared at Ao from within the carrier. She was frightened.

This was no place for animals. Seeing the cat tense up, Ao knew she needed to take her away. It felt like the cat was telling Ao: *Take me with you.*

But she couldn't actually hear the cat's voice. That was Ao's own desire speaking to her. It was she who wanted to take the cat with her.

She held the carrier with both hands. As she rose, her eyes met the doctor's. She was confronted with his plain, unremarkable face again.

"Take care," the doctor said.

When she emerged from the examination room, she saw a man seated in the chair that had been empty when she had arrived. When she saw his face, she was startled.

The man looked just like the doctor she had seen moments ago. Sure, he had the kind of unremarkable face that was a dime a dozen, but she had not expected to encounter another one in the same space. But their demeanors were utterly different. The doctor had been giggly and dubious; this man seemed somber. He was also staring at her with a puzzled expression.

"Ms. Torii, over here."

A pale hand waved at her from reception. The nurse was peering at her from the window. A sense of unease spurred Ao toward her. She handed over the note from the doctor, and the nurse produced a paper bag. Inside were food and a litter box.

"So, these are for the five days?" Ao asked.

"There's an instruction leaflet inside, so please read it carefully. Take care."

Ao was not one to chat, but the nurse struck her as cold. Ao rummaged through the paper bag. There was the bare minimum of supplies and a single sheet of paper. She pulled out the paper to read it.

> **NAME:** Shiro. Female. About four years old. Khao Manee. Feed a moderate amount of cat food in the morning and at night. Water bowl must always be full. Clean kitty litter as needed. She is very cautious. Make sure to clean areas where she could hide, including corners and spots behind furniture, in advance. If she does slip through a gap, do not force her out—use food to lure her. Please keep her clean, as dirt causes her stress. That's all.

Ao couldn't take her eyes off the leaflet.

Shiro. My Shiro.

The nurse was busy with administrative work at her desk and seemed unconcerned. After they handed the cat over to her, it was no longer their responsibility, and it was as if Ao were a stranger. This was not a good place for cats. Ao clutched the carrier to her chest as she walked out.

Like Matsuo, she had to return the cat in five days. *Will this unit still be a clinic then, or will it be an empty space? Or will it revert to being Nakagyō Ni-Nies?*

The thought frightened her. She wanted to release

Shiro from the cramped crate as soon as possible, so she hurried home.

When Ao opened the door to her studio apartment, her breath caught in her throat.

The room was littered with boxes filled with clothes and manga books she had brought with her when she moved out of her family's house. She had planned to sort through them eventually, but she had forgotten they were even there.

Shoot. She bit her lip. When looking for an apartment, she had only cared about finding a place close to a train station and had not considered its size. If she had known a cat would join her, she would have thrown out everything she didn't need. There was only a small space by the kitchen—just enough for one person to stand—where she could put the water and food bowls and litter box.

But if it was for just five days, they should be able to manage. Many people who lived in small apartments kept cats. It wasn't impossible.

She placed the carrier on her bed. Shiro's nervous energy was palpable. Ao, too, was thrown by the sudden turn of events.

"Shiro."

Ao opened the pet carrier's door and peeked in. Cats were wary animals. They needed time and space until they trusted you. Ao knew this, but she couldn't stop herself from taking a look. She wanted to bond with Shiro again. She wanted to brush her white fur and make it nice and clean. She leaned in, wanting to see those gold and blue eyes.

It happened in a split second.

Shiro leaped and rammed into Ao's face. Ao fell back, lost her balance, and tumbled off the bed. In the commotion, a cardboard box toppled off the wardrobe onto the floor.

"Ouch . . ."

She clenched her teeth and pulled herself up. She'd landed hard on her rear, but she wasn't injured. When she saw the box on the floor, a shiver went down her spine—what if it had fallen on her head?

What if Shiro is caught underneath it?

"Shiro?"

Shiro was nowhere to be seen. Ao crawled on the floor and searched every corner of the apartment. She rummaged through her trash can and turned over her bedsheets and curtains.

There was just one room in the entire apartment—

where could she be hiding? Ao looked between her towels and even turned her shoes upside down. She even checked inside her saucepan, but there was no sign of Shiro. Given her white fur, she should be easy to spot, yet Ao couldn't find her anywhere.

Ao stood motionless in the middle of her apartment.

A faint electric hum came from her mini-fridge. It was pushed flush against the wall, leaving no space. Still, just to be sure, she pressed her cheek to the wall—and there, wedged in the narrow gap around the wiring, was a white ball of fur.

"You have to be kidding me . . ."

How could she have got in there? Cats were able to defy the laws of physics somehow. Shiro had curled up her body and forced herself into the gap. Her white fur was pressed directly against the back of the fridge and the electric cords—it was dangerous.

"Shiro, come here. That's not safe."

Ao knew Shiro wouldn't come out even if she called out to her. This had happened several times at Nakagyō Ni-Nies. The more you reached toward the cat hiding behind the shelf, the farther it scooted away. It was a hassle. The only way to get it to come out on its own was to lure it with something irresistibly tasty.

Ao looked through the paper bag the clinic had given her. She found one tube of lickable treats. It was as if they had predicted this situation.

"What the heck . . . that's annoying."

She felt she had been manipulated by that doctor and nurse, and it irritated her. The moment she tore open the tube near the refrigerator, Shiro began stirring. It was the smell. Though not as keen as a dog's, a cat's sense of smell was still pretty sharp. Shiro clambered out, coated with every last speck of dust from the gap.

This was probably going to be the start of a game of chase. Shiro licked the treat, crouched low and ready to bolt. Once she was done, she would surely dart off somewhere again. A cat could be kept even in a small space like a studio apartment, but only if the environment was correctly set up.

Shiro clung to Ao's fingers, trying to lick every last bit of the treat. She was so absorbed in her delicious snack she had forgotten to be wary. Her breath was rapid and desperate. Ao felt Shiro's soft, moist paw pads on her fingers.

A smile and tears appeared on Ao's face. Fragile and adorable. Earnest. Ao thought about what she could do for Shiro now—the things she hadn't done back then.

She had people she could ask for help, but she hadn't reached out to them.

Ao grabbed her phone with her free hand. The treat was almost all gone, but she didn't want to let go of the cat just yet. Doing her best not to move the hand Shiro was gripping, she made the call.

She should have asked for help a long time ago—a long, long time ago.

Her sister, Midori, answered the phone. It had been three years since Ao had heard her voice.

"Hey, Sis."

Ao was briefly distracted as Shiro moved away, but she stayed nearby, licking her mouth. Like any cat, she instinctively cleaned herself after eating, stretching her tongue to wash her face and paws methodically.

It was Misato who'd told her that cats who spend time grooming themselves do so because there's no one else who will do it for them. Had no cat in Shiro's life wanted to fuss over her and keep her clean?

She remembered Shiman, who had continued to groom Miiko despite Miiko's hard punches. While cats are typically solitary creatures, felines who grow up together tend to be supportive of one another, despite occasional squabbles. Cats' understanding of personal boundaries was unlike humans', which sometimes led people to mistakenly believe they were distant or cold. But they were not like that—the cats at Nakagyō Ni-Nies had taught her that.

The cats had loved one another.

Yet they had been pulled apart.

As Ao chatted with her sister, her hands instinctively drifted to her neck. There was no necklace. The doctor had told her to stop being angry, but what she had felt was anger at herself. Now, there was no necklace to keep her in check.

"Sis, I want to come home. I don't know how long I'll stay, but I need help caring for a cat. Can you talk to Mom and Dad for me? I . . . I don't know . . . how to negotiate the distance between us, so I'm afraid I'll end up scratching them again."

And hurting them.

Midori, on the other end of the line, was gentle and calm. There must have been many things she wanted to say, but she listened to what Ao had to say first. She would likely act as a go-between for Ao and their parents. Ao was able to rely on her because she knew that.

As soon as she hung up, Ao sprang into action. Shiro kept shaking and grooming herself, clearly unhappy with her dust-covered fur.

When Ao stood up, sensing her presence, Shiro ran off again. This time, she hid under the bed. She would probably come out covered with dust again.

Bathing a cat unused to humans was nearly impossible. Washing little Shiro in the sink had been challenging, and it had taken hours, even with Misato's help, for Shiro to be completely dry.

There were many things Ao could do alone. If she tried her best, it would work out.

But sometimes, she needed help. Shiro, who was currently hidden, needed help from others. To keep her fur clean, Ao's support alone wasn't enough.

She opened the pet carrier she had brought from the clinic. It was unlikely that Shiro would get into it easily.

So she had to do what she had to do. What she could do.

She would go home, taking Shiro with her.

A week had passed since that strange doctor had prescribed Ao a cat. She went to return her uniform at the restaurant where she worked part-time. When she looked around the dining room, Matsuo came over.

"Are you quitting, Ms. Torii?"

"Yes."

Ao could have quit over the phone. She could have returned her uniform by mail. But she wanted to thank Matsuo one last time.

"I was only able to get to the clinic because of you. Thank you."

"Thank *you* for everything. I think it's because you were with us that I was able to take Fuku-chan home. If I'd been on my own, I don't think I could've made a decision."

"How is Fuku-chan? The same?" asked Ao.

There were still several bandages plastered on Matsuo's arm. There was a faint red scratch on her cheek.

"Hmm. She hasn't accepted me at all. But that's okay. I've learned something from Fuku-chan's caution," Matsuo said. "I have to admit, I've always thought of myself as easily liked by others. Presumptuous, right?" Matsuo giggled.

Matsuo was meticulous in her work, personable, and always smiling. Ao didn't know whether people liked her or not, but she had a favorable impression of Matsuo. But in Matsuo's wry smile, she saw a hint of sadness.

"Among the moms at Yua's kindergarten, one is very cold toward me, and I've been trying to understand why. I thought maybe I'd done something to make her dislike me, but I realized it's because I tend to assume others like me, and don't notice when they are being reserved. It's not about their liking or disliking people; some just take time to open up. In the first place, not everyone wants to be friends—you have to take into account compatibility and different family situations. Fuku-chan helped me see this. Maybe Fuku-chan and that mom will never be close to me, but I'll greet her whenever I see her, and I hope to be able to pet Fuku-chan eventually. Even if I can't do it right away, I want to close that gap bit by bit."

For Ao, who was used to keeping her distance from others, Matsuo's sentiment was hard to understand. Being on guard felt comfortable for Ao.

"But what if you can't close the gap? With the cat?" Ao asked.

"Then, I'll just get more scratches. The scratches on your arm, those are from a cat, too, right, Ms. Torii?"

Ao had told Matsuo about how she had been prescribed a cat at the Nakagyō Kokoro Clinic for the Soul as well. Both of Ao's arms were wrapped in bandages.

Adhesive strips and gauze alone couldn't cover the extensive wounds.

"Yes. When I put her in the bath, she threw a huge fit," said Ao.

"You live alone, don't you? Isn't it hard to bathe a cat by yourself?"

"My sister helped me."

Half of her wounds were from when she had put the dust-covered Shiro in the pet carrier, and the other half were from when she had washed Shiro in her family's bathroom. With Midori's help, she had scrubbed Shiro with cat shampoo. By the time they'd finished chasing her in circles to rinse her, the shower hose had been hopelessly tangled. They'd wiped her down with a bath towel and finally dried her with a hair dryer.

It had been a real ordeal. Not only did bathing drain the cat's energy, but it could also damage the trust between owner and pet. That was why keeping them in a clean environment was so important. They needed a spacious area where they could move around freely, and it was essential to have someone to help if something went wrong.

To get all those ducks in a row was challenging, and so Ao had decided to move out of her apartment. She'd find a pet-friendly place soon, but for now, she and Shiro would stay with her family.

Over the previous three years, Ao had had little contact with her parents. Their relationship had never been strong, and she had doubted they would accept her easily, so she had asked Midori, whom they trusted, to serve as a mediator.

Her parents had been surprised and unsettled when Ao came back with a cat. They had been skeptical that she could adequately care for it. In the past, even a slightly displeased look would have led to a clash. But to secure a place for Shiro, Ao would not run.

"Are you going back to return the cat at some point?" asked Matsuo, seemingly concerned.

She's a kind person, Ao thought. She closed her eyes and shook her head. It was five days past the return deadline.

Ao had lost the necklace. There was nothing for her to be cautious about anymore, but that didn't mean she should forget her anger. She still could not forgive herself for not doing anything back then.

For that reason, she was going to keep Shiro by her.

She wasn't sure if there would ever be a day she'd feel ready to return Shiro.

There was no sense of time here.

Nikké was staring up at the ceiling in the examination room. As he sat cozily in the warm space, he thought it would be okay if he closed his eyes and didn't open them again. Yet he found himself opening them anyway. Staying awake was harder. It was brutal to fight against the pull of sleep that threatened to drag him under.

He had no idea how the dull examination room appeared to the patients. But it was the same everywhere. Loved ones were everywhere. If you wanted to see them, you could do so anytime. The only reason people didn't was because they chose not to.

The silver necklace wrapped around his hand glimmered in the light. Within its capsule pendant was a cat's baby tooth. The person who had left this behind would not return.

The curtains behind him parted, and Chitose entered. By the time he thought, *Oh no!* her cold glare was on his hand.

"You're playing with it again."

"No, I'm not. I'm just wondering how I can call out to the patient who won't come back here . . ."

Chitose thrust out a hand, and Nikké narrowly dodged it. Chitose struck again, throwing rapid jabs like a boxer unloading a flurry of punches. Her speed was astonishing.

But Nikké wasn't about to lose either. He grasped the necklace tightly as the back-and-forth continued.

Before long, Chitose stood up straight and resumed her usual composed expression.

"That's not fair. Let me play with it, too."

"I'm not playing with it. This is precious to the patient, so no. I'm going to hide it now," he said, stuffing it into his pocket.

Chitose let out a disgruntled snort.

"That's why I told you that cat was too strong for that patient. What are we going to do? She might not come back."

"That's a problem. We can't stay here forever. What can we do to spread the word about our clinic? Should I be more stylish? Maybe I can grow my hair or get a perm?" said Nikké.

"Whatever you do won't work, because the raw material is uncool. More importantly, if we spread the word, other patients might sneak in as well. Don't doze off—stay sharp, okay?" With that final pointed jab, Chitose vanished behind the curtains.

Nikké opened his palm. The necklace had become warm.

"You've been waiting, haven't you?" he said. "Let's wait a bit more. I'm sure she'll come again."

The owner of this necklace was huddled in loneliness, unable to share her feelings with anyone. The image made Nikké's heart ache. He clenched the necklace once more.

His spirited little sister was still at an age where she wanted to play, and anything that jangled was a temptation. He decided to hide the necklace somewhere she couldn't find it.

He heard voices outside. It seemed that someone had wandered in. If you ambled through the streets of Kyoto long enough, alleys appeared unexpectedly. The door was always open, and whether you opened the heavy door was up to you.

An elderly woman walked into the clinic. She seemed taken aback to see the cramped examination room and Nikké seated at a desk. What people were worried about varied from person to person. These worries had different shapes and colors. But cats could solve most problems.

Nikké smiled broadly.

"We'll prescribe you a cat. Chitose, please bring the cat."

Reaching the fifth floor, Akira Shiina deliberately took his time walking down the hallway. He quieted his steps even more as he approached *that* unit. He moved silently, like a cat.

"This is dumb. Why do I have to act like a cat?"

It was unlike him to be scared. In the first place, he had no reason to be. He walked back to his office with his typical, confident stride. Meows and cat fur were of no concern to him. Whatever was happening in the unit next door, it had nothing to do with him.

He sank into his chair dramatically and threw his legs up onto his desk. Business had not been great lately. Sales were creeping along, but rising supply costs were eating into his profits.

Thinking about cutting costs was pointless—he was the only employee. At one point, he had considered moving because he didn't like the neighboring unit, but the rent in this building was lower than in most others. There was nowhere else to trim expenses.

"I guess I'll have to increase my prices . . ."

He let out a deep sigh. Raising his prices would lose him customers. But if he did nothing, the low margins would cause the business to fail. Shiina was in his late thirties. He had moved from job to job over the years, having seen countless shops and businesses go bankrupt due to poor management. With small businesses, one moment of carelessness could lead to their instant collapse.

"Or should I stick with it? We might stand out more if we don't increase prices now. The rent here hasn't changed either, so I'm inclined to stay."

He suddenly noticed that it was unusually bright. He turned around and saw that the blinds behind him were raised. The cleaning woman must have forgotten to lower them.

From the window, Shiina looked out at Kyoto's pale sky. The building itself was a bit sketchy, but the location wasn't bad. It was close to the shopping district yet still quiet. In any case, now was not the time to move.

As he was about to lower the blinds, he noticed a silver necklace near the window frame.

"What's this? Did the cleaning lady drop it?"

It was a simple necklace with a stainless-steel capsule pendant. The chain was thin and short—likely a woman's necklace. Shiina held it up to the window.

"Hmm. Lockets and capsules. People wear them for a reason, right? Something meaningful and magnetic . . . Memories that ease shoulder pain . . . An aging society that walks with memories . . . Not a bad phrase, I'd say."

An idea came to him. He hung the necklace on the latch on the window frame—the cleaning woman should notice it when she came by to clean again. He lowered the blinds.

The rent in this building was cheap. The location wasn't bad either. But the neighboring unit was too iffy. Even now, if he strained his ears, he felt like he might hear something.

"All right! I can't play it safe. I'll go on the offensive, turn it all around in one shot, and say good-bye to this weird building! Let's go!"

He wouldn't have anything to do with the next-door unit anymore. Whether someone was imitating a cat or if a real cat appeared, he was going to ignore it all. He was also going to stop being scared. If he heard meowing again, he'd meow back at the top of his lungs.